The Stolen Street Girl

NELL HARTE

©Copyright 2021 Nell Harte

All Rights Reserved

License Notes

This Book is licensed for personal enjoyment only. It may not be resold. No part of this work may be reproduced in any form or by any electronic or mechanical means including information storage and retrieval systems, without written permission from the author.

Disclaimer

This story is a work of fiction, any resemblance to people is purely coincidence. All places, names, events, businesses, etc. are used in a fictional manner. All characters are from the imagination of the author.

NELL HARTE

Table of Contents

Disclaimer..iii

Chapter One..1

Chapter Two 13

Chapter Three 27

Chapter Four 31

Chapter Five...45

Chapter Six 51

Chapter Seven..61

Chapter Eight 75

Chapter Nine...79

Chapter Ten 87

Chapter Eleven.......................................91

Chapter Twelve 99

Chapter Thirteen 109

Chapter Fourteen 117

Chapter Fifteen 125

Chapter Sixteen.....................................131

Chapter Seventeen 139

Chapter Eighteen *153*

Chapter Nineteen *161*

Chapter Twenty *167*

Epilogue *179*

PREVIEW *185*

The Little Chimney Sweep Girl 185

Part One *187*

Chapter One 187

Subscribe to Nell Harte's newsletter and receive Subscriber only books. ***201***

Chapter One

A hot summer wind blew across the peninsula of the Isle of Dogs, bringing the earthy stench of decay, the rot of wood, and the sour sting of dead fish. Ada Blair flared her nostrils, so used to the pungent smells that she barely noticed them anymore. Her slight, undernourished frame crouched in the mud like a furtive marsh creature. Indeed, it took a keen eye to notice her, for she had camouflaged her face with the foul sludge of the riverbank, to protect her already sunburnt skin from the rest of the day's glare.

It won't be long now. She trailed her fingertips in the scum-frothed water, waiting for it to recede a little further to reveal the morning's unpredictable catch. Her dark eyes glanced from side to side, making note of her competitors; the other eager mudlarks who were gathering on the riverbank. Up and down the Thames, she knew this scene would be echoed. Desperate hands clawing and scraping through clods of filth for the city's waste, praying to find treasure amongst it.

"Have ye caught a whiff of somethin', Sis?"

Ada turned to see her two brothers approaching, with their mother not far behind. Though, in some ways, Ada was more of a mother to those boys than the woman who had given birth to them. At ten-and-four, she made sure their faces were washed, their clothes were darned and scrubbed, and their bellies did not gnaw too badly from starvation, while their mother wandered through London for as many hours as it took to sell the day's haul.

"Well?" Jacob, the elder of the two boys at ten, prompted. "How's yer magic nose this mornin'? Any rubies as big as a duck's egg in the mud?"

Joshua, just turned seven, squealed with glee. "Rubies?!"

"Hush now, boys, else ye'll have everyone runnin' over to our spot," their mother warned in a hushed tone, as she set down three woven mats and a basket for herself and each of the boys. Ada had brought her own. She always set out early from their lodgings further inland; a cramped back room on the structurally questionable second floor of a filthy, disused warehouse. For the cargo that came into the nearby docks, it should have been a prime location for storage, but the foundations had succumbed, not long after it had been built, to the sucking and sinking force of the marshland that this 'island' had been claimed from.

Ada turned her dark eyes back to the gradually retreating tideline. "I saw a few sparkles and glints, so I'm hoping today might be a lucky one." She kept her voice quiet, heeding her mother's prudent warning. Mudlarks were merciless when it came to getting their hands on the best finds, and she had seen children and women beaten to within an inch of their lives for far less than a precious jewel.

While Ada's mother arranged the mats and the baskets, the two eager boys came to sit on either side of their sister, not caring about the mud slicking the seats of their trousers. Why would they? Since the day their father died of pneumonia, almost as many years ago as Joshua had lived on this Earth, they had all become entities of the marshland, with brackish water in their veins and muck forever underneath their fingernails and in their hair.

Jacob glanced up at her with the hazel eyes he had inherited from their father. "Did ye really see somethin' shiny down there?"

"Now, don't go getting your hopes up. You just focus on staying in the shallows with Joshua and picking up as much driftwood as you can." Ada ruffled his russet-brown hair, flecked with the coppery tones that all the children had taken from their mother and father. Though Ada's hair was as fiery as scrap copper. Indeed, she was more like her mother than either of the two boys. Although, these days, her mother's long, red curls were interspersed with coiled, wayward greys that seemed to multiply as the seasons passed.

Joshua pouted. "Why do I have to stay in the shallows?"

"Yeah, all the good stuff is further out," Jacob added stubbornly. Since turning ten, for some reason, he had become more insistent about being the 'man of the house,' and being treated as a grown up. But, to Ada, he was, and would probably always be, just a child who needed protecting.

Ada sighed. "You know why. It's dangerous further out." She pointed to the barges and vessels that were slowly making their way up and down the river.

A constant flow of water traffic; filled with potential peril.

"You could get hit, or you could get stuck in the mud, or you could get caught in the currents underneath the surface and be swept all the way to the sea."

"I can swim." Jacob puffed out his pigeon chest.

"You can thrash about. It's not the same thing," Ada retorted, with a smile. Through the lean months, the winter winds that made their warehouse home almost colder than the outside world; the injuries from broken glass in the mud or afflictions from the marsh air in the summer's heat or swallowing a mouthful of the foetid water where bloated animal carcasses could often be found bobbing, the family still stood together as an unbreakable quartet.

Jacob shook his head effusively. "I *can* swim. Ye just haven't seen me do it. I been practicin' really hard."

"Still, you're going to stick to the shallows," their mother chimed in, her tone stern. "I'll not have what happened to Etta happening to any of you."

The boys turned solemn, whilst Ada turned her sad gaze out toward the shimmering miasma that danced off the murky river. Sometimes, at dawn, when she came down here to secure the family's spot, she would watch the mist rolling across the ever-moving surface and imagine she could see her little sister's spirit in the eerie fog.

A ghost, serving as a warning to all of those mudlarks who became too bold with Mother Nature, and took too many chances with the riptides and fickle currents.

We all miss you, Etta. I know it's been two years, but I still wake up some mornings and expect to find you curled up against me, all warm and sleepy, like a little kitten.

She knew that Jacob missed their sister in a way that none of them could understand, for she had been his twin. Together in the womb, growing up side by side, they had shared everything, including two fiery tempers that would have them sparring one minute and hugging the next.

And when Etta died, Jacob did not speak for weeks. Indeed, they were all worried that he might not recover from the awful blow of her loss. But then, one day, he turned to Ada and said, "I'm hungry. Can I have some bread and butter?" After that, though Ada knew he would never forget his twin, he had returned to some semblance of normality.

"I could've saved her if I'd learned to swim back then," Jacob muttered miserably, kicking a hermit crab into the silty water. "If Pa were around, he could've taught us all, and then... she'd be here."

Ada put her arm around Jacob's shoulder. "It wouldn't have done no good, little bug. Even the best swimmers would've struggled against that wave. Ma can swim like a fish, but there was nothing anyone could've done to make it right. Etta was too far away from the shore."

"It's all Pa's fault." Jacob stuck out a trembling bottom lip, his hands balled into fists in an attempt to prevent tears from falling. "If he hadn't got sick, we wouldn't have had to come here. We wouldn't be mudlarks. We'd be safe in Hackney: you, me, Etta, Joshua, and Ma."

Joshua crawled around Ada and snuggled into his elder brother. "Don't be sad, Jacob. Ada saw shiny things. It'll be a nice day."

Ada scooped the two boys closer, wishing she could take away all the hardships and pain that the Blairs had endured, and the two absent presences that they all still grieved in their own way.

"It wasn't Pa's fault, either. It wasn't anyone's fault," Ada said softly, fighting to push away the memories of that day.

You were too far out... It was raining too hard, and the current was too strong... I told you to come back in to the shore, but you thought you'd seen something under the water. You wanted a big prize because we were hungry, and we hadn't eaten much for weeks. You were desperate... And then the wave came, and it dragged you off your feet. You disappeared... Ma dove in after you. I screamed and grabbed Jacob, so he wouldn't try to go after you. Ma searched for an eternity, until her lips were blue with cold, but... you were gone. She couldn't bring you back. In the end, it was the tide that brought you back, like one of the lost treasures we search for every day...

The truth, of course, was far less poetic. Ada and her mother had risen early every morning after that tragic day, to wander the shoreline as far as their legs could carry them, hopelessly scouring the riverbank for any sign of Etta's body. It meant setting aside their daily toil, but that did not matter. Only putting that dear, sweet girl to rest mattered.

They found her on the fourth day of looking, tangled in some barbed roots that protruded like a skeleton's claw from the muddy embankment.

To Ada's horror, it certainly looked as though her little sister had been immersed in water for four days. In fact, they were only able to recognise her from the yellow ribbon that had somehow managed to stay in her coppery hair.

As mother and daughter, the two of them had buried the child a short distance from the riverbank, with a large stone as a grave marker, so they would not forget that final resting place. Painstakingly, Ada had etched 'Etta' into the rock with a knife, for the names of her family were just about the only words she knew how to spell. They had thought about taking her back to the Isle of Dogs to bury her in a proper churchyard, but the poor little girl's body was so damaged and disfigured that they had not dared to carry it so far, in case it disintegrated all together.

"Remember boys—dart in and dart out, quick as you can, and don't let any of these other wretches take what's yours." Ada's mother brought everyone back from their quiet contemplation. She looked to Ada. "And don't you go in past your waist if you can help it, my girl. I don't like the look of the water over there." She pointed to a particularly murky spot in the river, where the water moved strangely, in almost smooth whorls, and silt swirled beneath the surface, warning of temperamental currents beneath.

Ada had been so invested in thoughts of Etta, and in clutching her brothers to her, that she had not noticed the throngs that had arrived on the peninsula. Hollow-cheeked, desperate-eyed people crowded and jostled to get as close to the water's edge as possible, ready with baskets and sacks for their, as-yet undiscovered, wares. Children were pushed closer to the front, weaving around the legs of the adults to get a better spot.

"And watch out for the barges and the boats," Ada added a warning of her own. Having business of their own to attend to, the river folk would barely bat an eyelid if their vessel struck a mudlark.

After all, they were seen as the vermin of the riverbanks, stealing the waste that the city had already thrown away.

Fortunately, with so much spiny gorse and a jagged mosaic of shells and broken-up rocks surrounding them, the position that Ada had selected remained relatively devoid of people. She had an eye for the best locations, and a nose for the best finds, though the Blairs kept that to themselves, for fear it might draw the other mudlarks to their chosen spots.

Ada got to her feet and retied her hair with a ribbon, so her fiery hair would not get in her eyes. "Come on, then. Time and tide wait for no man, and they definitely don't wait for us mudlarks."

Focusing on the glinting dot she had seen in the filthy water, she picked her way across the spiky ground and dug her toes into the slippery, slimy mud as she entered the water. Along the bank, she heard the thud and groan of people falling onto their backsides, unfamiliar with the give and shift of the liquid mud beneath their feet. But she held fast, with the grip of a seabird or an otter, and waded deeper into the Thames.

The air filled with the sound of splashing and the occasional bark of pain as the sole of a bare foot met with a shard of broken glass. Ada did not hear much of it. When she entered the water, her mind had a way of drowning out everything but the sensations around her feet, and of her hands dragging through the river like a net. Feeling for treasure.

"Ugh!" Joshua's tiny voice shrieked, prompting Ada to turn.

"What's the matter?" she asked.

Jacob picked up a lump of matted, rotten fur by what might once have been a tail. "I think Joshua found a fox."

"Well, throw it away and don't touch your mouth," Ada's mother instructed from the riverbank, where she stayed to keep watch over any goods they might discover. Mudlarks could be ruthless by nature, thinking of themselves first, as so many in London were forced to do. The Blairs had experienced thefts before, and they were not willing to take that chance again. They did not earn enough from their meagre haul to be able to lose a single piece of driftwood, or coal, or scrap iron.

Ada turned her attention back to the subtle glint in the water, barely visible to the naked eye through the layers of shadow that swarmed around her. Across the river, hundreds more gathered on the banks and waded into the river, but they did not concern her. To get to where she was, they would have to swim a considerable distance. And surprisingly, considering the environment in which they worked, not many mudlarks knew how to swim.

Please be worth something... Ada clenched her toes into the muck of the riverbed, feeling the gelatinous squelch. When they had first begun this business of scavenging in the dirt, the sensation had made her stomach churn, and the scents of the foetid river had been so overwhelming that she had thrown up into the water more times than she cared to count. Now, none of it bothered her.

Let it be an old boot, so we can get some leather out of it, or a silk handkerchief that'll fetch a pretty penny. Even a bit of copper would do the trick.

The boys were looking skinnier than usual. Just that morning, she had poked her head around the threadbare sheets of fabric that served as their partition curtain, to wake them. Jacob had thrown his blanket off in the night, revealing the painfully indented runnels of his ribcage, and the near-concave dip of his stomach. Joshua was little better, though she knew Jacob slipped him more of his own meal when he thought no-one was looking. Truly, she wanted nothing more than to be able to buy a few scraps of meat to put into their evening broth, in the hopes of fleshing her brothers out a bit.

Her foot pressed on something hard in the riverbed. Like a monkey, she curled her toes around it and brought it up through the water, where her hand was ready to bring it out into the open. A moment of anticipation, before the offering revealed itself.

Slowly, she unfurled her fingers and a small smile crept onto her lips. She had struck gold on her first scoop of the morning: a sawn-off length of copper pipe, about as long as her index finger and twice as wide.

"You'll do nicely," she whispered, before slipping it into the oilskin pouch at her waist. An item she had fashioned herself after finding a full coat of the stuff a few months back. Perfect for storing her muddied winnings.

"Hey!" Jacob's voice made her turn sharply. "Get off that, ye little river rat! I found it first!"

Behind her, in the shallows, her brother wrestled with another urchin; the two boys playing a brutal game of tug of war with what appeared to be a silk handkerchief.

Anger spiked through Ada's chest.

Tying the fastening on her oilskin pouch, she waded quickly back through the water to her brother, fully prepared to give the sneaky thief a lesson in ownership.

"Oi!" she barked.

The thief, who looked a few years older than Jacob, flashed her a sour look. "Stay out of this, woman. This ain't got nothin' to do with ye."

"Actually, it does." Ada brought the side of her hand down on the boy's wrist. "That's my brother you're stealing from, and if you try something like that again, I'll dunk you in the water until you learn not to take what ain't yours."

The boy yelped in shock and loosened his grip on the handkerchief, giving Jacob the chance to yank it free and hide it in his pocket. "It ain't yours, neither," the boy protested, as he massaged his wrist. "None of this stuff belongs to anyone."

"If you find it, you keep it," Ada retorted. "If you take it from someone who found it, then it's stealing. Now, get away from here before I decide to dunk you anyway."

The boy scowled at her. "I'm goin' to make ye regret that."

"Same goes for you if you don't skedaddle!" Ada warned.

With his lips twisting up into a grimace, the boy backed off, retreating further up the curve of the peninsula. All the while, his eyes shot daggers at Ada.

Watching him leave, she could not help but wonder if she might have reprimanded someone she should not have. Without their father, her family were more vulnerable than she would have liked to admit, and crossing the wrong person could spell disaster for them all.

Chapter Two

Giddy from yesterday's collection of driftwood, copper fragments, the hard-won silk handkerchief, and a decent handful of nails and discarded iron, Ada hummed cheerfully to herself in the hazy dawn light that splintered in through the warped wooden panels of their warehouse home. Her mother had fallen asleep by the fire, after a lengthy evening turning those cast-offs into solid coin, but the small purse on the kitchen table looked pleasingly plump.

"My girl," her mother murmured sleepily, evidently awoken by the quiet humming. "You're like a cockerel, always waking before the sun comes up."

Ada chuckled. "Someone's got to get the boys awake, and I can't expect you to do it, can I? You barely sleep as it is." She nodded to the purse on the table. "I take it you had a good night."

"Not too bad at all," her mother replied, rubbing her eyes. "Let's hope today is just as bountiful, eh?"

Ada nodded. "Our spot is the best on the river. It's on the right curve, you see, so a lot of the stuff that washes down from the city gets caught there." She tapped the side of her head. "It's all about knowing the lay of the land."

"I never thought you'd be so good at this, Ada." Her mother did not sound proud. If anything, she sounded sorrowful, like she wished she could change the way things were.

Ada shrugged. "I suppose I got used to it."

"Yes... I suppose we all did." Her mother got to her feet and dusted off the greyish skirts of her timeworn dress. "Now, why don't you get the boys up whilst I put together something for breakfast. There's not much tea left in the tin, but there should be enough for two cups if you want one?"

"Thank you, Ma." Ada walked up to her mother and planted a kiss on her cheek, before heading back through to the back room where the boys slept behind their partition. Halfway there, she thought she heard a strange sound coming from behind her, in the kitchen: a sob, softly stifled.

I'm sorry, Ma. I know this isn't what any of us wanted. But, like so many others of their lowly class, they had no other option to persevere and survive.

Fed and watered, all four of the Blairs made their way from their ramshackle home to the familiar expanse of the peninsula. Dawn had risen about an hour ago, and it would be another hour before the tide receded. As such, the Blairs would have to wait until it was safe to begin their daily toil, but Ada did not mind that.

Sometimes, the best moments she shared with her family were upon the riverbank, whilst they waited for the water to expose its nightly draw.

Ordinarily, Ada would go ahead of her family to make sure their spot was secured, but her mother had looked so weary this morning that she had stayed to help prepare breakfast.

"That's our spot!" Joshua pointed a tiny finger to the patch of gorse and marsh weeds which they usually preferred to use as their base.

Ada squinted into the gloom, to find several shadows already lurking there. Three of them, though it was hard to be sure, thanks to the fog that continued to wisp up from the river.

"We can't lose our place," her mother said quietly, in a concerned tone that frightened Ada. "We've got rents to pay and food to buy, and what I made yesterday will barely cover this week's costs."

"I can just find us another spot," Ada insisted. The air felt too still, and even the lapping water seemed to be whispering a warning not to approach the shadows up ahead. True, it may have been the best location along the peninsula, but they could scrape enough at a different position. Ada just needed a moment to sense the way the wind was blowing, and to observe the river's currents, to pinpoint a potentially lucrative bit of riverbank.

Her mother shook her head. "You told me this morning why that spot is the best, and I won't lose it to some newcomers who don't understand the way things work here. We need this spot. You found copper *and* a silk handkerchief yesterday. That's worth holding our ground for."

Ada opened her mouth to protest again, but her mother had already marched forward, weaving through the prickles of the gorse bushes. Panicking slightly, Ada grabbed her brothers' hands and led them after their mother, though she did not know what they could do if this turned nasty. Even Jacob, at ten, was small for his age, and these shadows looked much, much bigger than any of her family.

"Morning to you," her mother said to the furtive figures, whilst Ada held onto her brothers.

At least she's treading carefully. After all, she supposed her mother was the professional when it came to genteel negotiations, for she negotiated every single day for the best price at which to sell the day's collection.

The three individuals who had commandeered the Blairs' spot turned in unison, and Ada's chest clenched with a newfound swell of fear. A haggard old woman with rheumy eyes, a nest of tangled grey hair, and a grizzled scowl, stared back at Ada's mother. Flanking her stood two tall, broad-shouldered boys wearing the same savage scowl upon their pocked and dirty faces, though they were really closer to men than children. Ada guessed they were perhaps ten-and-six and ten-and-eight respectively, though the older of the two had furrows across his brow that belonged to someone more weathered in years.

"Aye," the gnarled woman said haughtily. "Morning to ye an' all."

Ada's mother squared her shoulders. "I've not seen you around here before."

"So?" the woman replied.

"So... you might not understand how things work." Ada's mother put one hand out; a subtle gesture, as if to say to her children: "Keep back. Let your ma deal with this."

The elder of the boys snorted. "And ye're goin' to tell us, is ye?"

"We've been working this riverbank for years, and this is our patch," Ada's mother shot back, her voice firm yet fair. "If you're new, you find your own spot further down the river. You don't come by one day and push your way onto someone else's ground."

The younger of the two folded his arms across his chest. "Aye, well we found us a spot 'ere and we int leavin', so ye best be findin' yourself a new place down the river."

"That's not going to happen." Ada's mother took a step forward.

"Teach 'em a lesson, lads," the haggard woman instructed with a cold, twisted smile. "Make sure they dint bother us again."

Ada edged near to her mother. "Ma, maybe we should—"

"I'm not giving up this spot, Ada," her mother hissed back. "We can't afford to."

The elder boy cast a lecherous eye over Ada, making her skin crawl in a way that even the silty, slimy riverbed had never been able to provoke. "Mayhap ye should listen to yer lass, whoever y'are."

"And maybe you should listen to me."

Ada's mother stepped forward with a length of lead piping in her hand. Ada had no idea where her mother had drawn it from, but there it was, black and crusty and ominous in the still-fuzzy morning light.

The younger boy gave a low whistle. "Now that ain't too friendly, is it?"

"I'm warning you. Get off my family's patch of ground!" Ada's mother raised her voice, though her daughter could see how much she was trembling. Over the years since Ada's father had died, his wife had been forced to learn how to defend herself and protect her family, but sometimes the enemy was just too big and too powerful.

"Nah, that ain't goin' to happen." The elder boy lunged forward in the blink of an eye, his hand curled into a fist aimed directly for Ada's mother's face.

Thinking fast, Ada leapt forward a split-second later, and pushed her mother out of the way, only to take a glancing blow to the shoulder. A piercing pain ricocheted down her arm and across her chest, taking the wind out of her sails. She staggered for a moment and gripped her toes into the earth to stop herself from toppling over from the immense impact.

"Don't ye touch our sister or our ma!" Jacob howled.

Before Ada could stop them, her brothers darted past her and flung themselves at these usurpers. She watched in horror as the younger of the rough-looking wretches tossed Joshua away as though he were a ragdoll, the little boy flying into a barbed thicket. Meanwhile, the elder wasted no time in delivering a chilling punch to Jacob's face, that sent her beloved brother reeling back, like a reed bending in a storm.

"I'll see you drowned for that!" Ada's mother roared, as she lumbered into the fray with the lead pipe still in her hand, desperate to protect her sons.

"Ma, no!" Ada screamed in reply, as she ran to help. She knew they were outmanned, and would have given anything to be able to drag her mother away from this, but her mother was too strong, burning with a violent rage that could not be tempered.

Everything happened in a blur of fists and shouting. Ada's mother tried to swing at the elder boy with the lead pipe, only for him to duck back at the last second. Whilst her mother was recovering from the momentum, the wretched creature landed a blow. Ada wished she had not heard the awful sound of a neck whipping back, and prayed it was only the sound of warped wood cracking, but there was no denying that her mother was injured.

"Ma, come on. Please, we have to leave here," Ada begged, as she watched her mother stumbling around like a dazed inebriate in the streets. The dark glisten of blood trickled out of her mother's nostrils, and more leaked from a cut to her lip, the oozing substance dripping down her chin.

Just then, the younger boy wrenched the lead piping out of Ada's mother's hand and raised it as though he meant to strike. Swallowing her terror, Ada skirted in front of her mother and put up her hands.

"Don't!" she rasped. "We'll go, just... don't hurt her."

The elder of the two reached for the raised pipe and tore it out of his brother's hand.

With a smirk upon his cracked and scarred lips, he banged the pipe against his palm and eyed Ada with that same lecherous intensity. "I'd be willin' to let ye share in this spot, for a price. It wouldn't cost ye more than ten minutes of yer time."

Ada's stomach roiled with nausea. "It'd cost me far more than that, whoever you are. But just know, there's a curse on this river. It punishes those who don't respect it, and those who don't respect the people who work here." She held his gaze defiantly. "And I hope it punishes you, in the worst possible way."

Turning around, she grasped her mother's flailing arm and pulled it over her shoulder. She knew she should not have antagonised the elder boy with that last statement, but she could not help it. Even if she could not pummel him with her fists, she could at least leave him with a haunting warning, and hope it came to pass.

"Jacob, get your brother," Ada instructed, her heart aching for the two boys. Joshua limped slightly on his right leg as he untangled himself from the spiny thicket, whilst Jacob's face was already beginning to swell from the punch he had endured. Still, they were a strong, courageous family, and her brothers showed their bravery as they put their arms around one another and walked away from the riverbank.

A short time later, they were back in their two-room lodgings above the sinking stilts of the warehouse, tending to their wounds. Ada, being the only one who had not received any injuries, cleaned up Jacob's split lip and Joshua's grazed skin as best she could, using her fingernails to pincer out some of the thorns that had pricked the latter.

With that done, she had sent them back to bed to rest. Though, in truth, she had ulterior motives for gaining some privacy with her mother.

Picking up a damp cloth, Ada scraped her chair closer to her mother's, and began to dab at the swollen lip. "We're not going to be able to work today, Ma. Maybe not for a few days, whilst those folks have still got their blood up." The greyed fabric took on a hue of pink. "I'll go along the riverbank in a couple of days and find us another spot."

"It won't be enough," her mother muttered grimly. "Our rents and our vittles were relying on a good week, Ada. If we can't work for a few days... it won't be enough."

Ada forced a smile onto her lips. "What do you mean? We've got a decent amount from yesterday's sales. That purse looks plenty fat to me."

"It's not. Check it." Her mother looked away, shamefaced.

Puzzled, Ada reached for the purse and opened the drawstring, before tipping the contents out onto the table. To her utter disappointment, only four pennies and a large handful of copper nails clattered out onto the splintering, unvarnished wood.

A moment later, the silk handkerchief also tumbled out in a soggy, dirty ball, where it slowly began to uncurl from its crumpled state.

So, that's why the purse looked full...

"But... you said it was a good night of selling," Ada whispered, suddenly very scared.

Her mother shook her head. "I said it wasn't too bad, and that was... a bit of a lie. No-one wanted to buy. No-one's been wanting to buy for weeks now. I thought the handkerchief would fetch a tidy sum, but everyone turned their noses up at it." She took the cloth and dabbed her lip of her own accord. "I can't get it any cleaner, and no-one wants a rust-stained bit of fabric that *looks* like it's been at the bottom of the Thames for months. No-one wants any of what we're selling, and I've tried... believe me, I have. Those four pennies were from your bit of copper, but the rest—I might as well have been trying to sell them plague rags."

Ada swallowed thickly. "What are we going to do? If we all go back down to the riverbank, we'll end up with more bruises, and maybe for nothing if things aren't selling. If I go back alone, I'll end up... I can't even say it, but I know what price that man wanted me to pay." She shuddered, having heard all of the horror stories and cautionary tales from her mother. "But... if we can't work, we can't eat, and we won't be able to pay the rents."

"I know," her mother replied quietly. "But I've got a thought that might prove useful."

Ada raised an eyebrow. "What?"

"I'm going to go out this evening, like I always do, and I'm going to... keep selling until I've made enough to see us through." Her mother cast her a weighted glance that suggested there was more to this idea, but Ada knew better than to ask questions when she got that look in her eye.

Are you going to steal something, Ma? Are you going to pinch something valuable and sell it on?

Please, say that's not what you're going to do. All of the worst possible thoughts careened through Ada's skull, as she envisioned the police arresting her mother and throwing her into Newgate, or of the theft going wrong and her mother getting hurt in the process. Truly, she wished she could ask everything she wanted to, but her mother continued to give her that stern expression, rendering her silent on the matter.

That night, Ada sat by the meagre fire that she had built from the last of their scavenged driftwood. Her mother had gone out just as evening had fallen, and now the battered clock on the kitchen table showed four o'clock in the morning. Whilst that would not normally perturb Ada, she did not feel like she could rest until she had made sure her mother returned safely.

The smoke billowed from the hearth and stung at Ada's eyes, making her feel even sleepier.

"I won't fall asleep. I won't," she told herself, repeating the sentiment over and over in the hopes that it would make a difference. For it would soon be dawn, and the boys would awaken shortly after that, and she did not want to have to tell them that their mother had not come home. It would be too much to bear, after the losses and struggles they had already been though.

Twenty minutes later, the sound of the door crashing open broke Ada out of her dozy stupor. Her mouth dropped open in alarm as she witnessed her mother stumbling into the larger of the two rooms, clearly drunk, and giggling to herself.

"Ma?" Ada got to her feet, her shock giving way to concern. "Are you all right?"

Her mother froze like a frightened rabbit, her glassy eyes squinting at Ada. "What are you still doing up?" she said, more accusatory than welcoming. "I told you not to bother."

"I wanted to make sure you came home in case you were in a gutter somewhere and I had to come and look for you!" Ada fired back, appalled by her mother's state. "Ma, have you been drinking?"

She shrugged. "A tipple, maybe. I'd say I've earned it after the life I've had."

"Did you sell anything?" Ada almost did not dare to ask, for it looked as though all of her mother's coin had gone on gin. The nickname 'Mother's Ruin' had never seemed more appropriate.

Her mother staggered to the table and sank down, lolling like a sailor on turbulent seas. Somehow, she managed to fumble the coin purse from the neckline of her dress, and promptly hurled it at Ada.

"I got us another sixpence, actually."

Ada caught the purse and tipped the contents onto the table. Three pennies clattered out. "Then where are the other three?"

"I don't know," her mother replied laconically.

Ada scooped up the coins and put them back into the purse. "I think you do. I think we both do." She swallowed a swiftly forming lump in her throat. "You should get yourself to bed before the boys wake. I don't want them seeing you like this."

"Well, don't you go waking me." Her mother grinned oddly as she lumbered back onto her feet, and swayed toward the back room, where a partition separated the boys from the mats where Ada and her mother slept. "I've nothing to get up for, so you've no reason to disturb me."

You're the one that's disturbing me, Ma. Ada bit her tongue and watched her mother go, terrified that this was an omen of more hardships to come. Her mother had been so strong for so long; it had only been a matter of time before she snapped.

Chapter Three

Blank-eyed and exhausted to the point where nothing seemed real anymore, the days and nights blended into one endless lesson in waiting and worrying for Ada. Her mother left their lodgings late in the afternoon and did not return until the wee hours, where she proceeded to sleep through until the afternoon again, rising only to eat the paltry offerings that Ada scraped together with the sparse coin they had left.

"Where's Ma?" Joshua shuffled up to Ada on the seventh day of her mother's wayward antics. He put his little arms around his sister's waist and held on tight.

"She's out selling again," Ada half-lied, for she did not know what her mother did when she left the lodgings, aside from the drinking. Sometimes, she returned with a few coins. Sometimes, she returned with less than she had gone out with.

Jacob slid onto one of the kitchen chairs, his face sour. "Is Ma sick?"

"She's not feeling like herself, that's all." Ada offered her brother a smile, and fluffed Joshua's hair.

"Is that why she's sleepin' all the time?" Jacob pressed. He was no fool. He knew something was amiss, but Ada did not have the heart to tell him the truth: that their mother had taken leave of her senses, or the blow to her head had knocked something in her mind out of place.

Ada nodded. "Yes, little bug. She just needs some rest, then she'll be all right again."

"We should have soup!" Joshua suggested brightly. Being so young, he was less aware of the dire situation.

"Soup?" Ada tried to match his enthusiasm.

Joshua nodded eagerly. "When people are sick, they eat soup."

"Then, why don't I see what I can make?" Ada did not know whether to smile or cry, for she already knew that they did not have much in the way of food. "How does… cabbage soup sound?" She ruffled Joshua's hair again and forced herself to smile with all her might. For him.

Joshua chuckled. "Cabbage soup will be good!"

"Jacob, can you help Joshua cut up that cabbage while I see what else I can find?" Ada cast pleading eyes at her other brother. She could see he was angry at their mother, but they had to maintain appearances for Joshua, as well as their own dwindling morale.

Jacob shrugged. "Come on, Joshua. Let's pretend this cabbage is a rabbit and get it skinned and ready for the pot."

Thank you, Ada mouthed.

He nodded with a sad smile.

With the boys distracted, Ada padded over to the door of their lodgings, intending to go down to the docks and beg some scraps from anyone who would take pity on her. She opened the door and was about to step out, when a familiar figure stopped her.

"Ah, Miss Blair. Is your ma at home?" Daniel Forbes, the landlord, flashed a cold smile. A mean-faced creature with a meaner spirit, Ada always dreaded seeing him anywhere near their lodgings. Even when her mother had the money for rents, he made a point of bandying threats and warnings around, so the payments would never be late.

Ada swallowed thickly. "She's not, Mr. Forbes. Did you want to speak to her? You can tell me, and I can pass it on to her."

"I s'pose it don't matter which one of you I talk to, so long as you're out of here by Monday morning." Daniel leaned against the doorjamb.

"What?" Ada wondered if she had misheard him.

His smirk turned nasty. "Your ma hasn't paid your rents for over a month, now. She begged for more time and I gave it, which you know I never do, and for good reason." His eyes glinted with irritation. "She still didn't pay 'em. That means she owes me two months, and I ain't waitin' for my coin no more. So, you tell your ma that she either coughs up two months by tomorrow, or I want you out by Monday morning. I think we both know which way that's goin' to swing, eh?"

Ma... why didn't you tell me it was this bad? Desperation swelled in Ada's chest as Daniel waited impatiently for a reply. Not that he really needed one.

"Please, Mr. Forbes, could you just give us another week to find the money? I'll bring it to you myself," she begged. "Think of my brothers, sir. This isn't their fault."

Daniel reached out and tilted Ada's chin up with his dirty forefinger. "I told you; I ain't waitin' no more. Bring the coin by Sunday or be out of here by Monday. That's the end of it." He flicked her chin, his nail catching her skin, and turned to walk away. Ada wanted to get on her knees and beg for leniency, but she knew Daniel Forbes. He would not be disappointed twice, nor would he repeat the leniency that he had already given to her mother.

Ada closed the door and leant against it, breathing hard. In the kitchen, she heard the steady chop of the boys cutting up the last cabbage they had. Tears pricked at her eyes as she sagged down to a crouch and rested her face in her knees. To a wealthier gaze, these lodgings might not have seemed like much. But these two rooms were home; the first place they had settled after their father died. Now, come Monday, they would have to bid its security farewell.

"Where will we go, Ma?" Ada whispered miserably. "What's going to happen to us?"

She did not have an answer for either question.

Chapter Four

Three days of aimless wandering began to take its toll upon the Blair family. All four of them carried their sparse belongings as if they were nomads in a foreign land, praying for some charitable soul to give them a place to sleep for the night. The first night, they slept under a tree in a churchyard. The second, they were allowed to take refuge in the church itself. The third... they huddled together at the entrance to an alleyway, where the boys curled up and dozed off like vagrant cats. Even their mother managed to rest after gulping down a jarful of gin, but Ada did not sleep a wink. She was too fearful that someone might snatch one of the boys or try to attack her and her mother.

"Can we eat today?" Jacob grumbled on the morning of the fourth day.

Ada tried to blink the perpetual grit out of her eyes. "We might have to go back to the church and ask for some soup and bread. Would you like that, Joshie?"

The littlest of the quartet had ceased to speak after the churchyard. Something had spooked him in those terrifying shadows, but he would not, or could not, say what.

As such, he did not answer Ada. He simply stared at the opposite wall of the grimy, dark alley.

"Where's Ma?" Jacob asked, his tone heartbreakingly harsh.

Ada sighed, feeling the weight of the world on her narrow shoulders. "I don't know, little bug."

Their mother's belongings were exactly where she had left them, alongside the empty jar of gin that had numbed her into slumber. Ada had asked her mother where she was going, when the older woman had suddenly awoken and got to her feet, not long after dawn, but her mother had refused to respond.

She's probably gone to get more of her Mother's Ruin... She hated that she had come to think such things of her mother, whom she loved dearly, but their former matriarch had transformed into someone that Ada did not even recognise. As if her mother had been swapped for a changeling, whilst those vile young men on the riverbank had distracted the rest of them.

"Is this our life now?" Jacob lowered his gaze, and Ada saw his shoulders shaking.

"I... don't know that, either," she admitted, wishing she had better news for them.

Jacob kicked a stone, and sent it skittering up the alley. "I wish Ma had died instead of Pa."

"Don't say that!" Ada scolded instinctively. "Ma isn't well, that's all. She'll be better soon, and *we'll* be better. I promise."

Jacob raised his head and hit his sister with a fierce scowl.

"Ye can't promise that! I might not be full grown yet, but I know that ain't medicine." He aimed a second kick at the empty jar of gin, his scowl deepening as it smashed against the far wall.

"Jacob, you just need to have faith in Ma." Ada knew she was asking a lot. "Her head got injured when that fella hit her, but she'll be back to herself when the bruises have gone."

He snorted. "Ye don't have to talk to me like I'm a wain. I'm not stupid."

"I know you aren't," Ada replied softly. She was about to offer more words of comfort, when a shadow stretched across them, disrupting their conversation. To Ada's surprise, when she looked up, she found her mother standing there with a proud smile upon her face.

"Get your things together," she announced. "We've got ourselves a place to live."

Ada raised an eyebrow. "We do?"

"I wouldn't lie to you," her mother retorted, more defensive than was necessary. "Now, come on, unless you want to spend another night here."

Terrified that such a thing might actually come to pass if they hesitated, the three siblings all gathered their belongings and followed their mother to this mysterious new residence.

~ ~ ~ ~ ~

Ada was nothing if not a pragmatist, but she had not expected the cramped, dismal conditions they had ended up in.

The warehouse had been damp and unstable, but at least there had been space for all four of them.

Now, they were forced to share one tiny room in the area of Shadwell, with oily-furred rats and mischievous mice as their bedfellows.

"Aren't we lucky?" their mother insisted, as the days turned into weeks, and the heat of summer took on an edge of biting autumn.

Ada always smiled and responded with a cheerful, "Of course we are, Ma."

It was not entirely untrue. There were others in the city who did not even have the luxury of a rotting roof over their head, and Ada knew that they would survive the winter, thanks to the woodstove they all slept beside. It was not much, but at least they would not be one of the frozen corpses loaded onto a death cart when it snowed, having died of exposure in their sleep.

"Remember to be home before nightfall," Ada instructed, some six weeks after they had come to live in their new lodgings. Joshua smiled up at his sister with a mouthful of bread crust, whilst Jacob fetched two makeshift broom from the far side of the room.

"We will," the latter replied.

Ada put a hand on her hip. "I mean it. It's not safe outside when it's dark."

"Ye worry too much." Jacob flashed her a grin and beckoned for his younger brother to join him, so they could proceed with the day's toil.

Joshua had still not spoken since they were forced out of their home on the Isle of Dogs, but he seemed more cheerful in himself. At least, that was Ada's hope.

"Someone has to," she replied, with a smile.

Jacob ruffled his younger brother's hair, and the two boys left the fusty, restrictive room they now called home, but not before Jacob turned to bid his own warning to his sister. "Keep yerself safe an' all, Sis. I saw some odd'uns out on the street yesterday. They was pesterin' some other girls, 'til I chased 'em off."

Ada nodded. "I will."

With them gone, she finally allowed herself a moment to sit at the small wooden table, to scavenge the last of the breakfast scraps. In the right-hand corner of the room, barely ten paces from where Ada sat, her mother slept so deeply that a thunderstorm would not be able to wake her.

Are you sure we're lucky, Ma? What about you? Ada watched the curled-up figure with a heavy heart. Life, these last six weeks, had not turned out too badly for the Blair siblings. Joshua and Jacob kept busy in the streets, earning a modest sum from sweeping the horse manure off the cobbles, taking on any labour tasks that were offered, and performing tricks for passers-by. Meanwhile, Ada had turned her scouring talents to suit the land, hunting through the gutters and alleys the way she had once hunted through the river mud.

But their mother... Well, there were only so many choices presented to a woman of the lower classes, who needed to make as much coin as possible, as quickly as possible.

These days, she drank her gin to erase the memories of her nightly acts, and slept most of the day for the same reason.

"I'm sorry, Ma…"

The foetal figure stirred beneath her blankets. "What for, my girl?"

"Ma? I-I didn't mean to wake you!" Ada stood sharply, as though she were about to salute to a general. "Go back to sleep. Don't mind me."

Her mother pulled herself up into a sitting position. "I'm awake now." She rubbed her sleepy eyes. "What were you saying sorry for?"

"It doesn't matter," Ada insisted, furious with herself for speaking out loud. After all she endured to keep this roof over their heads, her mother deserved an uninterrupted slumber.

Her mother canted her head. "Are you worried about me? You can be honest. The boys aren't here to overhear."

Ada swallowed uncomfortably. "Sometimes. I mean, you're out all night, meeting… strange men. Anything could happen to you."

"It won't," her mother promised.

"I just… I just wish you didn't have to do what you do," Ada continued, her cheeks burning. "You shouldn't have to… um… sell… you know. It's not fair."

Her mother chuckled. "Jacob's right: you worry too much."

"But you could search the gutters with me, instead. You could do something else, and then you wouldn't have to be a…"

Ada trailed off. Even now, she could not bring herself to use the word 'prostitute.'

Her mother stretched out her long, slender arms. "It's not so bad once you get used to it, my girl."

She paused: her expression somewhat vacant. "After all, your father and I did the same thing many, many times to make all of you."

"That was different," Ada protested. "You loved Pa. You were married to him."

Her mother's expression clouded over, and she lay back down, pulling the blankets to her chin. "I'm tired again, my girl. I'm just going to sleep awhile longer. Make sure you leave a few scraps for when I wake up."

You miss him. We all miss him. Every day they spent here was a reminder of how far they had fallen from the life they had once had. Of course, they could pretend everything was fine, and distract themselves with their respective work, but Ada only had to look at her mother to feel the past creeping back into her mind. Taunting her.

Once upon a time, they had lived in lodgings with three rooms, on a more desirable street in Southwark. Their father had made a decent sum as a stevedore, whilst her mother had worked at a sewing house until she fell pregnant with Joshua. Every day, Ada would take Etta and Jacob down to the docks to sell scraps of cloth that her mother had pocketed from the sewing house, to add a few extra coins to their income. After their father died, the owner of the sewing house refused to employ their mother again, thus forcing them into the mudlark business.

"I'll be back at two o'clock, Ma," Ada said, as she gathered her shawl and basket, and headed for the door.

Silence echoed back.

Leaving her mother to her private grief, Ada hurried down two flights of rickety stairs and stepped out into the tepid morning, where a glum sun beat down upon the city. London was already abuzz with people bustling to-and-fro, and the cries of costermongers, selling their wares from rattling barrows, pierced the thrumming air.

Ada walked to the end of the crowded street and turned right onto the river path, making for the sordid underbelly of Soho. There, she knew she would have her best chance of finding cigar ends, discarded without care. For those who smoked cigars did not know how valuable the remaining tobacco in those ends could be. Some days, they earned her a penny apiece. Tuppence if there was plenty tobacco left.

Kensington, Belgravia, and Fitzrovia were also on her list, but those parts of London came with the risk of being chased away by constables.

On her way to Soho, she kept an eye out for anything else she might be able to sell: bits of cloth, stray ribbons, broken chunks of coal, and animal bones. It amused her to think that she had become a veritable rag and bone woman, for that mode of employ was usually reserved for men with sizeable carts and sacks. Still, it allowed her to earn without drawing too much attention to herself, or the ire of those true rag and bone men.

Following her usual path, which she walked day after day, mile after mile, she veered off toward Russell Square.

There was one stop she needed to make before trawling through the labyrinth of Soho: Thomas & Son's Stonemasonry.

Please say Mr. Thomas has some cigar ends for me, she prayed as she approached the workshop.

I could use a victory today. The stonemason had become something of a surety for her in the past few weeks, mostly thanks to his love for smoking cigars and his son, who never failed to stash the ends away for her.

The small bell over the door jangled as she entered. A gossamer snowfall of stone dust covered the floor, echoing her footprints as he headed for the counter. In the workshop behind, she heard the familiar grate and grind of stone being shaped and smoothed.

"Ada!" A young man of ten-and-five popped up from under the counter, wearing a cheerful smile. "You're late this morning."

Ada smiled back. "The boys took a while to eat their breakfast. I think they were trying to avoid sweeping horse manure for as long as possible."

"Who'd blame them?" The young man, Elijah Thomas, son of Harvey Thomas, chuckled the easy chuckle of someone who had never had to struggle much in their life. She envied him that. But whenever she came here, and spent time with the sandy-haired, blue-eyed boy, with his youthful face and ready smile, she felt her woes slough away like water off a duck's back.

"Are you sure you can't apprentice Jacob here?" Ada asked the same question every day, hoping she might be able to prod at least one of her brothers into better prospects.

Elijah offered her a familiar look of apology. "I would, but you know what my pa's like. He doesn't want anyone in that workshop who isn't blood. Sometimes, he doesn't even want me in there."

"I know that's not true," she replied shyly. "Your work is beautiful."

"You think so?" He brushed a hand through his curly, fair hair.

She nodded and pointed to one of the examples in the window. "I've never seen a prettier gargoyle."

"Ah, that's actually a grotesque."

Ada frowned. "Huh?"

"A gargoyle funnels water away from a roof, but a grotesque is just decorative. My pa won't let me do a gargoyle just yet, in case the funnel part doesn't work." He leaned on the counter, his blue eyes twinkling.

Ada rested her basket beside his folded hands. "I learn something new every day."

"How are the boys, anyway?" Without saying a word, Elijah took up a sharp-looking pair of scissors and cut away a loose bit of reed that had come away from the basket. It had been spiking Ada's arm for days, but she had not dared to try and deal with it.

"Joshua still isn't talking, but they both seem happy enough. They've got food, they've got a place to rest their heads—what more do you need?" Ada tried to put on a façade of good humour, but all she could think about was her mother, curled up in the corner of their tiny room, trying to fight off reality.

Elijah toyed with the cut-off piece of reed. "And what about your ma?"

"Same as ever," Ada replied stiffly. "How's your pa?"

He shrugged. "Belligerent."

She did not expect Elijah to ask after *her* father, for he had already learnt, the hard way, that it was not a happy tale.

"I could come by with some leftover stew, if you like?" he said unexpectedly. "There's always too much for me and my pa, and you might not have to go looking for so many odds and ends if I helped you."

Ada did not know what to say. She had never been too proud to beg, when it came to her family's welfare, but there was something about charity that left her feeling uncomfortable. As if she were somehow being pitied. Of course, she knew that was not Elijah's intention, but she also knew she could not accept.

"That's kind, but we're not doing too badly for ourselves, and I honestly do like the work I do. It gets me away from our lodgings and it lets me come in here to speak to you every day," she replied, her cheeks warming. "I suppose searching the streets reminds me of better days."

"When you were mud-larking about?" He flashed a grin, evidently taking no offence to her refusal.

She nodded. "Do I sound mad if I say that I miss it?"

"Not at all," he assured. "I'm an earth creature—I like stone and rock. You're a water creature, and that's where you thrive. It makes perfect sense to me."

Ada canted her head. "I've never thought about it like that before."

"Like you said, we learn something new every day." He laughed softly and gestured to her basket. "I take it you're here to collect some hidden treasures?"

"If you have some," she replied.

Elijah ducked back down behind the counter and stood back up with a small box in his hands. "There might not be any tomorrow, but my pa went through two and half yesterday." He lifted the lid to reveal the goods, and Ada's eyes widened with glee.

An entire half! Lucky days were few and far between, but that made her all the more grateful when one finally blessed her. She could easily get three or fourpence for so much remaining tobacco, even without the other two stubby ends.

"Doesn't he want to finish this one?" she asked, as she transferred the treasures into a handkerchief at the bottom of her basket.

Elijah tapped the side of his nose. "He fell asleep with it in his fingers, and I snuck it away. What he doesn't know can't hurt him."

"Thank you, Elijah!" Ada could have embraced him if there was not a counterpane between them. "This is exactly what I needed today."

He gave a mock salute. "Happy to be of assistance, Miss Blair."

"I don't want it to look like I just came here to get these, but I really need to be on my way." Ada cast him a shy smile. "I have to be back home at two o'clock, so I don't have much time for my street-larking."

Elijah pushed the basket toward her. "I hope you have a fruitful day, Miss Blair. And if you change your mind about that stew, there'll always be some here for you."

"Thank you, Elijah." With a parting look of fondness, she took up her basket and headed for the door. Taking a breath, she reached for the handle and heard that comforting jangle of the bell overhead, before she stepped back out into her own harsh reality. For her fleeting moments in the stonemasonry with Elijah were nothing more than a brief reprieve.

Chapter Five

The seasons came and went; rolling through a frosty autumn into a stormy, bitter winter that made the Blairs glad of their woodstove. Though their lungs paid the price for that warmth, their throats itchy and raw from the black smoke that filled their cramped lodgings. Spring arrived with new, green buds that flourished into blooming flora and fauna, but London remained grey and unforgiving. A place where only the wealthy were permitted to blossom, whilst the perennial weeds of the lower classes struggled through an endless battery of starvation, sickness, and the constant threat of being tossed into the street.

As summer appeared on the city's horizon, Ada repeated the prayer that she sent up to the heavens week in, week out, come rain, sleet, or shine: *Let us earn enough to make a better life for ourselves. Give us that hope, I beg you.*

But no-one answered. No-one ever did.

"You look pale, Ada. Are you sick? Have you got enough to eat?" Elijah said, one July morning. Outside the stonemasonry workshop, the city's streets were hot as ovens, and the air had turned liquid, shimmering in the fierce sunlight.

Ada jolted her head violently, aware that she had been staring at the wall for a good few minutes, and had not heard a word that her dearest friend had said. "Hmm?"

"I said, you don't look well. Are you eating enough?" Elijah lifted the counter and came around to Ada's side. Without asking, he rested his palm on her forehead. "Well, you don't feel feverish."

She tried to blink away the sleepy grit in her eyes. "If I survived a winter, I can survive a summer. I'm all right, Elijah, I promise."

"You're skin and bone though." He eyed her with concern. "I've got kindling thicker than your wrists, and your dress is hanging off you like sackcloth."

Ada stepped back, so he would have to drop his hand. "We've had a lean couple of months, that's all. Spring was supposed to be our time to really earn some good coin but… we've barely scraped through."

"But your ma should be making a decent amount from the sewing house. Did something happen? Did she lose her employ?" Her mother's true employment was the one thing that Ada had not been able to tell Elijah, though she could tell from the curious look in his eyes that he knew something was amiss.

She lowered her gaze. "She lost some of her shifts at the sewing house, so she hasn't been making as much."

It was not a complete lie. Her mother *had* been making less and less money since winter. Or, rather, she had been spending the majority of her takings on gin.

That had meant less food on the table, less wood for the stove, and more work for the Blair siblings, in order to try and make up the deficit. Of course, given the nature of the siblings' employ, they had not even come close to matching their former income. Meals had been reduced to one solitary bowl of thin porridge or broth, supplemented by any scraps they could find in the gutters whilst they went about their daily business, and Ada dreaded the evening whimper of Joshua, as his empty stomach gnawed itself even hollower.

"Here." Elijah ducked back under the counter and produced a lunch pail. "Take it and give what you can't eat to your mother and brothers. I'm not taking no for an answer."

Ada turned her face away, so he would not see the tears glistening in her eyes. "What will you eat?"

"I'll just eat more at breakfast and dinner. Until your ma can get more work, you can come here every day and have my lunch." He picked up the pail and put it into Ada's basket. "Call it a gift, and you know it's rude to try and give a gift back."

Ada mustered a miserable laugh. "A year ago, I would've forced you to take it back, but... I'd be a fool to do that, now."

"We're friends, Ada. There's nothing I wouldn't do for you," he said, his tone so earnest that it cracked her heart.

She sighed softly. "I'll always be grateful for the day I met you."

"Do you remember it?" Elijah leant on the counter, propping his chin on his hands.

"How could I not? I tripped over right in front of you, and almost skinned my face."

This time, she managed a genuine laugh. "There were cigar ends rolling all over the street, and you crouched down and helped me pick them all back up again."

He nodded. "I asked what you were doing with so many, and you said you sold the tobacco for coin. So, I went inside and got about ten of my pa's smoked ends for you."

"And I've been hounding you ever since." She finished the story with a smile. Truly, in this past year, she did not know what she would have done without him. He had become her sanctuary in an endless war against landlords, her mother's fluctuating temper, and the hardship of literally having to scrounge a living from the streets.

"I wouldn't have it any other way." Elijah flashed her one of his brightest smiles. In that moment, she could almost pretend that everything was fine, and that her family was not falling apart at the seams.

She sank back onto one of the high stools by the counter. "I just wish I could get my ma to stop drinking. I've tried to reason with her and make her see how it's affecting me and my brothers, but I think it numbs her. That's why she won't give it up."

"Gin?" Elijah raised an eyebrow.

"It used to be, but now it's whatever she can get." Ada had to bite her tongue to stop herself from revealing the rest: that her mother sometimes sold herself for drink alone, if she could not get her buyers to furnish her with a glass of something for free.

Elijah reached out and took Ada's hand. "I'm so sorry."

"Me, too." She smiled sadly, for though she and her mother had argued time and time again about the drinking, her mother refused to promise that she would stop. Even though she knew that her children would go hungry without her coin to buy food. In truth, none of that seemed to matter to her anymore. *They* did not seem to matter anymore.

She's broken, Elijah, and I don't know how to fix her. In truth, Ada knew that no-one could. Her mother was too far gone.

Chapter Six

Ada stirred from her mat underneath the kitchen table, as the sound of cheerful humming filled the deadened stillness of the Blairs' lodgings. The boys were still asleep, snuffling softly in their corner of the room, oblivious to the strange noise. After all, judging by the hazy violet light outside the streaked window, it was not yet dawn.

Am I dreaming? Ada rubbed her eyes as the door opened and her mother breezed in, looking so joyful that it took a moment for Ada to realize who it was. She could not remember a time when she had heard her mother humming, and it had been over a year since she had seen the older woman wearing a genuine smile upon her painted lips.

"Ma?" Ada crawled out from under the small table. "You look happy."

Her mother twirled across the sparse bit of uncluttered floorboard. "I *am* happy, my girl."

"Did you make good coin last night?" Ada tried not to sound too eager, but her forever-growling stomach could not help but hope.

"I did," her mother chirped, as she laid her shawl on the kitchen table. "What's more, I've got myself a new employer and a lovely place to stay." She moved around the room as if she were floating, picking up her belongings and throwing them onto the shawl.

Ada stood excitedly. "We've got a new home?!"

"*I* have a new home," her mother corrected, with a wistful smile. "And I've got no time to be wasting. They're expecting me back within the hour."

Ada's body felt numb as she watched her mother continue to whirl about the room, collecting her worldly possessions so she could abandon her children. "Is this some kind of cruel jest? What do you mean *you've* got a new home. Aren't you taking us with you?" She tried to keep her voice as low as possible, for the sake of the boys, but it was proving difficult to suppress her rising anger.

"Oh Ada, don't be like that." Her mother wafted a hand through the air and dropped a small coin purse on the table. "That should pay for food for a few days."

"It's a brothel, isn't it?" Ada hissed.

Her mother did not reply, nor did she look at her daughter.

"You can't go to a brothel, Ma. You've got your children to take care of!" Ada dispensed with the attempt to be quiet, as her hands shook with disbelief.

"When you gave birth to us, you made a promise to be a mother, and now you're just... leaving? I know life hasn't been easy, but you can't walk away from us.

The boys began to rouse, but Ada did not care. If their mother was intent on this, then her brothers deserved to be witness to the woman's desertion.

"Maybe, if you stopped drinking, we'd be more comfortable. But if you walk out that door, you're sentencing us to worse than we've got now!" Ada spat the words. If her mother could look into her children's eyes and still walk out, then she might as well have been dead to them.

"Oh hush." Her mother laughed, as if this were something funny. "You'll all be much better off without me, not worse. I know I'm not doing what I ought to be, so I may as well stop being a burden to you all. This way, I can send money when I have it, without being a hassle."

Jacob sat up slowly. "What's going on?"

"Mama?" Joshua's croaky voice squeaked, startling Ada. The little boy had not spoken in a year, only to utter his first word as their mother was relinquishing her love and responsibility toward them.

Ada turned on her mother with renewed fury. "How can you be so cold? It's not about the coin. We're managing as we are. We want you to stay because you're supposed to be our mother. If you leave us now, you're nothing more than a coward!"

"Of course I am, my girl," her mother retorted. "That's why I have to do this. The decision has already been made."

Jacob got to his feet. "You're going? Are you coming back?"

"No, love." Their mother swept over to her eldest boy and tried to plant a kiss upon his forehead, but he pulled away sharply, his face transforming into a mask of disgust. "If you don't want to say goodbye to me, that's your choice. But I still love you all, and that won't go away, just because I'm not here." She did not try to kiss Jacob again. Instead, she crouched to stroke Joshua's cheeks and kissed his nose gently.

"Ma, think about what you're doing!" Ada shouted, as her mother came back over to collect her belongings. "Are they giving you as much as you can drink as part of the bargain? Is that why you're leaving?"

Do you really want to shut us out that much? Any pity she might have felt for her mother's plight evaporated. They had always been a family, pushing through every tragedy the world hurled at them. Now, their mother was breaking that bond, and reneging on a sacred covenant they had all silently made to one another when their father died.

Her mother shot her a dark look. "Now who's being cruel?"

"What else can you expect, when you're leaving us to fend for ourselves?" Ada spat. "I promised my brothers that you'd get better. I promised them you'd be yourself again, so you've not only made a fool out of us, but you've made a liar out of me!"

Her mother shrugged. "Then you shouldn't have made promises you had no way of keeping."

"Says you!" Ada felt as though her eyes were going to pop out of her skull, from the sheer pressure of the intense rage coursing in her veins.

Her mother bundled up the belongings and held them to her abdomen. "It'd be best if you pretended to the landlord that I'm still here. He'll boot you out, otherwise." She walked to the door, seemingly remorseless. "Take care of each other, and I'll send money when I can." She took one step over the threshold before turning back. "And try not to hate me too much."

With that, she was gone, and Ada did not have the strength or the impetus to try and drag her back. Why try and fight a battle that had already been lost? All she could do now was go to her brothers and hold them close, and try not to think about the enormity of the challenges that lay before them until they really had to.

"What did we do wrong?" Jacob whispered into Ada's shoulder as she hugged her brothers tight.

Her heart broke for him. "You didn't do anything wrong, little bug. She's the one who's making a mistake."

"Mama..." Joshua mumbled. Ada felt a dampness soaking through the sleeve of her dress, the fabric mopping up her littlest brother's tears.

"We're going to be all right," she promised. "I won't let anything happen to us."

Or am I just making another promise I won't be able to keep?

~ ~ ~ ~ ~

Reduced to a trio, the Blair siblings tried to make the best of their new, motherless situation as the months passed. With the help of Elijah's connections, the boys found more regular work as messengers, running goods and letters and parcels from one end of London to the other. The money was not immense, but it was enough to fill the gap their mother had left them.

In the meantime, Ada left the house at dawn and did not return until evening, using every hour God gave to scour the streets for discarded treasures. Even so, she knew they would not have survived without Elijah's well-timed 'gifts' of lunch pails and wax packages of 'leftover' meats and bread and cheeses, especially in those first weeks.

She was on her way to see Elijah, pulling her shawl closer about herself to fend off the autumn chill, when she turned a corner and almost ran headlong into a gentleman.

"Goodness, I'm sorry!" she cried, stumbling slightly as she fought to regain her balance.

The gentleman said nothing for a moment. He simply stared at her with curious brown eyes, set within an angular, handsome face. Dark curls framed his features, and a bluish wisp of smoke twisted up from a cigar as he lifted it to his full, somewhat feminine lips. The end burned amber as he sucked smoke into his mouth. A few seconds later, rolling white waves curled out of his lips, with a few tendrils puffing out of his nostrils, as though he were a mythical dragon.

Ada dipped her head and made to walk past him, when he finally spoke.

"What wares are you selling, Miss?"

She paused. "Pardon?"

"I asked what goods you are peddling," he replied, nodding to the basket that hung from the crook of her elbow.

"Oh... I'm not selling anything, sir. I... um... collect cigar ends," she explained, flustered. The fine manner in which he spoke signalled his wealth and status, and she could not understand why he would utter so much as a word to her.

He tilted his head to one side. "And why, pray tell, do you do that?"

"I sell the... um... tobacco." She tipped the basket so he could see the cluster she had already gathered that morning, from outside the gentlemen's clubs of Soho and Marylebone.

"How queer." His lips widened in a smile, as he suddenly stubbed the end of his cigar against the nearby wall. "You must have this, Miss. I had already grown weary of the flavour, but I did not wish to waste such a fine cigar. If you take it, it shall not be wasted." He held out the cigar, which had barely been smoked. If it were not for the blackened end, Ada would have thought it to be entirely new.

Ada raised a hand in protest. "I can't, sir."

"Why-ever not? You say you collect such things, and I am offering it freely," he replied. "I would be most disappointed if you were to refuse such a gift."

Ada smiled, thinking of Elijah. "I suppose it is considered rude to refuse a gift."

"Precisely!" He continued to hold out the cigar until, at last, Ada reluctantly took it and placed it with the rest of the day's findings.

"Thank you, sir. That is very kind of you," she said awkwardly, for he would not stop staring at her.

He brushed a curl off his forehead. "You know, you really are quite beautiful. I daresay I have not seen a prettier creature in all of London." His gaze moved across her face, like he was putting her to memory. "Exquisite skin, and such a delicate flush in your cheeks."

Her flush deepened at such an unwarranted compliment.

"I must know the name of my gift's recipient, and this rare beauty I see before me," he continued, apparently quite serious. "Do not ask me to guess, for I am terrible at it."

Ada gulped. "Um... Ada Blair, sir."

"Ada... Hmm, that is rather unusual. Indeed, it is perfectly fitting for such a unique young lady." His smile widened, the expression making his handsome face brighten. "As you have furnished me with your name, it is only right that I return the favour. Miss Blair, I am Stephan Beauregard, and it is a pleasure to make your acquaintance."

He took her hand and kissed it gently. Ada could only stand there in shock, wondering what on earth would possess a fine gentleman like this to kiss the hand of a nobody.

I don't like this. No, I don't like this one bit. His attention made her wary, and the fact that she had taken the cigar from him made her warier still. Wealthy folk did not give away anything without a price, and she feared what the fee might be for his generosity.

After he released her hand, she gave a polite dip of the head. "I'm very sorry to have knocked into you, Mr. Beauregard, and I'm grateful for the cigar, but I've got to be on my way."

"You have an appointment to keep?"

She frowned. "I've got to keep working, sir."

"Would you mind if I walked with you awhile? I have little else to occupy my time, and I should like to know you better, Miss Blair. It is not often a charming bird such as yourself happens to collide with me." He chuckled warmly: a sound that should have comforted her. Instead, it concerned her.

"I don't think I'm your sort of company, sir," she admitted.

His expression softened, as though sad. "I care not for social class, Miss Blair, if that is your worry? However, if my request has made you uncomfortable, then please forget that I asked. I am only interested in speaking with you a while longer, but I suppose I have little concept of the efforts it takes to do as you do."

"I just don't think I'm very interesting," she replied, scrutinising him on the sly.

If he had meant to harm her, or try and gain something from her, she supposed he would have made demands already. And there was nothing in his expression or his eyes that suggested malintent.

Indeed, now that she looked at him, he seemed almost as shy as her.

Mr. Beauregard gasped. "Then you must not see what I see."

He paused. "I promise, I shall only walk with you for as long as you care for my company, and I shall only speak to you until you grow tired of my questioning. Should that occur, you may ask me to leave you be at any moment, and I will heed your request."

"That would be... all right, I think."

He smiled again, his eyes lighting up. "Then show me the path that an industrious young lady takes through London."

As Ada began to walk along the street, Mr. Beauregard kept a polite distance, leaving a person's width between them. Only when they reached a much busier road, where horses and carriages clattered along without a care for those crossing, did the gentleman offer her his arm to help her safely to the other side. It was all the evidence she needed, that he wanted nothing more from her. Just someone to converse with him until high society called him away again.

"So, Miss Blair, tell me all about yourself," he prompted, as he resumed his gentlemanly distance.

Ada almost burst into hysterics. "Goodness, Mr. Beauregard, I wouldn't even know where to begin."

Chapter Seven

After that first, strange encounter with Mr. Beauregard, Ada presumed it had merely been a casual amusement, for him to pass an afternoon. So, it came as quite the surprise when she found him waiting on the same corner, the following afternoon, at exactly the same time. A cigar pinioned between his fingers, ready to add to her collection. After a week or so, she began to expect the sight of him.

"Can I ask you something?" she said, as he followed her along her usual refuse-picking route. He still maintained a polite distance, and they did not tend to speak of much, despite spending hours together: the weather, the horses and carriages that passed, and the occasional architectural treat that he liked to point out. As for personal matters, even on that first day she had not revealed much more about herself, aside from the fact that she was a small-scale rag and bone woman.

Mr. Beauregard cast her a curious glance. "Of course. The real question is, will I answer?"

"I wanted to know why you keep waiting for me," she replied. In truth, she still was not sure whether she looked forward to these late afternoon, early evening walks or not. He was pleasant enough company, and did not disrupt her work, but she could not fathom why a handsome, smartly attired gentleman, who must have been at least twice her age, continued to engage with her.

He shrugged. "You intrigue me."

"Why?"

He tilted his head to one side in thought. "You may find this difficult to believe, Miss Blair, but one can grow very weary of high society. There is a constant need to put on a façade, and to behave in a certain manner, and to always be aware of what one is saying and doing. With you, there is no need to be anything other than myself. I can simply walk with you and find a sort of contentment in watching the way you live your much… quieter life. You value what others would not look twice at, and I admire that."

"My life isn't really that quiet," she murmured. At home, she was expected to be a mother to two heartbroken boys.

He looked surprised. "No? Pray, tell me, what troubles your peace of mind?"

"I have to do all the work at home, whilst pretending to the landlord that our absent mother is still there. We have to be so careful, in case we're seen," she explained, encouraged by his engaged expression. After all, it was rare that someone listened to her woes.

"I've got food and rents and my brothers' health to worry about, and no idea what our future holds. Some days, I think we're happy, and we can keep being happy. Some days, I don't know if I can carry on as we are."

Mr. Beauregard nodded. "I cannot pretend to understand your plight, Miss Blair. I confess, I did not know matters were so dire for you." He paused. "Forgive me for asking, but is your mother no longer of this Earth?"

"Oh, she's alive, she just didn't want to be a mother anymore." Ada curled her hands into fists. "She was never the same after our father died, and it got worse after my little sister drowned, but I thought she'd at least want to stay with us and take care of the rest of us. Now, that's my role."

"I am so very sorry, Miss Blair." Mr. Beauregard dipped his chin to his chest. "That is quite awful. To look at you, I would never know you had endured so much heartache. Why, you cannot be very old, and yet you have lived a life with more tragedy than many experience in… say, five-and-thirty years of existence."

Ada bit the inside of her cheek so she would not cry at the softness of his tone. "I am but five-and-ten, Mr. Beauregard."

"And your brothers?"

"Eight and eleven, respectively," she answered, thinking of those dear boys. They would be returning home soon, eager for whatever paltry dinner she could muster from the vegetable tops, potato peelings, and beef bones that she had collected today.

Mr. Beauregard rubbed his clean-shaven chin. "Perhaps, if you would accept my assistance, I might be able to gain apprenticeships for your brothers. I would never be crude enough to offer you money outright, for I am always aware of wounding pride, but I should like to help in some capacity."

Ada stared at him in disbelief. "You would do that?"

"I would very much like to," he confirmed.

"But... why?" she gasped. "You barely know me."

He smiled. "I suppose you remind me of my nieces, and I would not be able to sleep of an evening if I thought you were out there, struggling terribly. However, as I said, I am aware that charity is not always appreciated, and you seem so independently spirited. As such, I should like to bolster you so that you and your brothers may help yourselves, rather than make myself some sort of wealthy saviour."

Ada said nothing for a while, as she contemplated his suggestion. Her dear Elijah had done everything within his power to help the boys improve their employment, and they seemed to enjoy running messages across the city. But she could not deny that she liked the idea of them learning a valuable trade, that would see them comfortable for the rest of their days.

What would you do, Elijah? I'll have to ask you tomorrow. She had not yet mentioned her encounters with Mr. Beauregard to Elijah, for fear that he might get the wrong idea, or that he might think himself inferior to the wealthy gentlemen. Of course, that was not true. Ada adored Elijah, and had hopes that, one day, their friendship might blossom into something more.

But she knew that pride and protectiveness could have a strange effect on men, and she was determined to tread carefully, so Elijah would not be touched by any green-eyed monster.

"You do not have to give me an answer right away." Mr. Beauregard broke the companionable silence. "The offer shall remain open."

Ada cast him a shy smile. "Thank you, Mr. Beauregard. And thank you for understanding that, despite what's happened to me over the years, I've still got a sliver of pride left."

"What would your pride say to a sumptuous dinner?" He gestured ahead. "I have a townhouse in Fitzrovia, not far from here, and I should like to ensure that you are well fed, for this evening, at least."

She paused in her tracks. "I've got to be getting back to my brothers, Mr. Beauregard. They'll be wanting their dinner soon."

"Then this is an ideal situation, Miss Blair," he enthused. "You may eat your fill, and I shall have my housekeeper prepare a hearty meal for each of your brothers, that you may take home to them. Perhaps, they would not mind waiting an hour or so longer, if they have the promise of such reward?"

They wouldn't hold a grudge if they could have some meat... Ada's mouth was already watering at the prospect of a rich stew, or a prime cut of beef, maybe with some creamy potatoes to go alongside. The boys worked so very hard, and she rarely had the opportunity to give them something in return for their toil, beyond what her own hands could forage from London's streets.

"It's tempting," she admitted, casting a glance down at the depressing collection of waste in her basket. Why would she feed her brothers a watery soup of vegetable bits and days-old bones, when Mr. Beauregard was offering something superior? A meal that could actually fill the void of their ravenous bellies, instead of simply taking the gnawing edge off.

Mr. Beauregard raised his hands in a gesture of peace. "Do not feel obliged. I will not take offence if you refuse. Nor is this my attempt to try and force charity upon you. Let us call it a... business meeting of sorts, where we can further discuss potential apprenticeships for your brothers, and perhaps a more fitting employ for yourself? I know of many houses that are always eager for industrious maids."

"Really?" Ada blurted out before she could stop herself.

If I can find myself a position in a good house, with a steady income, and my brothers can do the same as apprentices, we might have a chance of making something of ourselves!

Excitement thrummed in her veins, for this would be the first good thing to come their way, since the awful morning their mother had abandoned them.

Mr. Beauregard nodded. "I would not toy with you, Miss Blair." He hesitated. "So, what do you say? Would you like to partake in a business meeting with me?"

"I would," she replied, without pause. If this went well, her brothers would not only have meat for their dinner, but actual future prospects ahead of them. How could she refuse?

"Splendid!"

He offered her his arm in most gentlemanlike fashion, which she took with an awkward smile, before leading her toward his Fitzrovia townhouse and the meal she could not wait to devour.

No more than fifteen minutes later, they arrived outside an imposing building with a pillared porch and marbled front steps. Red and white roses bloomed in window boxes, and the imminent sunset turned the panes a molten shade of bronze.

Ada stared up at the house in awe, and a slight hint of apprehension. For the first time since meeting Mr. Beauregard, she felt ashamed of the threadbare dress she wore, and the holey boots that provided the merest barrier between her bare feet and whatever filth and muck and vague fluids lay beneath.

"I can't come into your house looking like I do, Mr. Beauregard," she mumbled. "I'm sorry. I should go."

He looked crestfallen. "Miss Blair, do you think I would ask you to dine with me if I held any judgement toward your attire or your character? I do not care a jot how you look. Although, if I may say, you could be clad in a sack and I would still find you the most intriguing creature I have ever beheld." His brown eyes implored her. "Please, allow me to nourish you and, by proxy, your brothers. Allow *me* to decide who is worthy to enter my abode and who is not, and you are, Miss Blair. Indeed, you may be the worthiest."

"Are you sure?" Now that she had the idea of a decent meal in her head, she did not want to relinquish it so easily.

He nodded. "I am quite sure, Miss Blair."

"I just... won't touch anything," she said nervously, as he ushered her up the steps and through the front door.

Ada's shame swelled to knee-trembling proportions as she set eyes upon a grand entrance hall, with a sparkling crystal chandelier, and more velvet furnishings than she had ever seen in her life. The drapes appeared to be genuine silk, embroidered with gold flowers, and there were paintings and sculptures to add character that were likely worth more than she could ever earn in a lifetime.

She was about to back away and run from the townhouse, out of sheer panic, when a kindly-faced older woman appeared from the left-hand corridor. Plump and smiling, the woman headed directly for Ada, and seized the girl by the arms.

"Aren't you a darling?" she cried. "But so malnourished! I can put my hand around your arms! Goodness, we must put that right immediately. I've a pot of beef stew bubbling nicely, if you'd care for a bowl? And I think we've some fresh bread that would be delicious with a thick slathering of butter." She flashed Ada a wink, her warmth putting the younger woman at greater ease.

Ada gave a feeble nod. "That'd be nice."

"Then you follow old Mrs. Chattoway, and she'll make sure you're treated like a princess!" The woman gently tugged on Ada's arm, urging her toward a room at the far end of the entrance hall.

Ada frowned. "Who's Mrs. Chattoway?"

"Why, that's me!" The woman cackled, as though she had told the funniest joke in Christendom.

Ada glanced back at Mr. Beauregard. "You won't be dining with me?"

I thought that was the whole reason for coming here. Her heart began to race, a doubt nagging in the back of her mind. What if she had made a mistake by accepting his offer?

He smiled warmly. "I shall join you momentarily, Miss Blair. I have some business to attend to with my manservant, and then we may begin our business meeting." He nodded to the door that she was fast approaching. "But please, do not stand on ceremony. If you have finished an entire bowl by the time I come to sit with you, I will not be remotely annoyed. I will simply encourage you to have another."

"Thank you, Mr. Beauregard." Ada's nerves ebbed once more, her week-long knowledge of the gentleman giving her renewed confidence in her decision to dine at this house.

True, she found it hard to believe that generous individuals existed in the upper echelons, but she had seen other such men helping the Christian Mission in the slums. Perhaps, his altruism was just on a smaller, more personal scale.

A few minutes later, she sat alone at a long, elegant dining table, illuminated by romantic sconces and three sets of candelabra that Mrs. Chattoway had insisted on lighting for the occasion.

The older woman had hurried out again, once Ada was seated, presumably to fetch the promised bowl of beef stew, and thickly buttered bread.

Don't be worried, boys. I won't be long. I'll eat, I'll ask for your food, and I'll be home before you know it. She fidgeted on the chair, unable to get comfortable despite the extensive padding beneath her backside.

Even when her family had resided in their three-room lodgings in Hackney, and had been invited to the local dances, she had never dined in such fancy surrounds. In truth, she did not quite know what to do with herself.

Fortunately, Mrs. Chattoway returned after a short absence, bearing a silver tray of delicious offerings. The heady aroma of the stew bombarded Ada's nostrils, even before the lid of the pot had been lifted, and she could not take her eyes off the gigantic slices of buttered bread that Mrs. Chattoway had arranged beside the main event. It thrilled her, to think that her brothers would be devouring this before long.

They'll sleep better than they have in months, maybe years, with that in their stomachs. A grin spread across her lips.

"Here you go, my dear girl." Mrs. Chattoway lifted the pot lid and ladled a generous portion into a separate bowl. "Now, make sure you take it slow. I don't imagine you've had much, and you'll be ever-so poorly if you guzzle it down like a gannet."

Ada nodded politely. "I will. Thank you, Mrs. Chattoway. This looks delicious."

"I do hope it is. I've been slaving over it all day." The older woman laughed and set the bowl in front of Ada, before taking the seat beside her. "Oh, and one of the kitchen maids is preparing two pails for you to take home to your brothers, per the master's request. I'll slip in half a loaf for them to share, too." She reached out and squeezed Ada's shoulder.

The gesture almost brought tears to Ada's eyes, for she could not remember the last time she had been shown maternal kindness like this.

Elijah never failed to give what he could to Ada and her brothers, but this struck her heart in a different way. This warm, welcoming, female presence was something she had missed, without knowing it.

"You're too kind, Mrs. Chattoway." Ada swallowed the lump in her throat and lifted her spoon to take her first bite of the thick, glossy broth, where a large cube of soft beef was just waiting to be tasted.

An explosion of flavour burst upon her tongue as she began to chew, ignoring the slight pain in her teeth. They had not had to contend with meat for months, and it showed. Still, she would not allow some mild discomfort to ruin this moment. Before she knew what she was doing, she was spooning up mouthful after mouthful, completely forgetting her promise to eat slowly.

"Ah, it's good to see a girl with a healthy appetite," Mrs. Chattoway encouraged.

Soon enough, the bowl lay empty before Ada, and only one slice of the buttered bread remained. She had used the soft, crusty chunks to mop up any remaining broth, until the bowl looked as though it had never had any stew in it, at all.

Sitting back in the chair, Ada rested a hand on her slightly distended stomach and basked in the joy of feeling utterly satisfied. Her limbs felt relaxed, her mind felt calm, and her soul felt as though it were at peace. All from one hearty bowl of stew. Indeed, as she let the back rest take her weight, her eyelids began to feel heavy, and a yawn stretched her mouth wide.

"Are you tired, dear girl?" Mrs. Chattoway asked, looking concerned, the way Ada's mother had once done.

She nodded. "It's only when you stop for a moment that you realise how exhausted you are."

"Then you should have a rest, before you have dessert with the master," Mrs. Chattoway suggested. "There's a bedchamber upstairs you can use, and I'll be sure to wake you after an hour or so."

"But... my brothers," Ada replied, her tongue slack and strange.

Mrs. Chattoway helped Ada out of her seat with remarkable strength. "They'll not be cross with you when they have a taste of my stew. You've earned a nice sleep, so don't you worry about those boys. You'll see them again soon."

Like a weary child, Ada followed Mrs. Chattoway out of the dining room, leaning against the older woman. Reaching the wide staircase, Ada lurched into the banister for support, her legs feeling shaky and her eyes oddly glazed, as though there was a cloudy film over them. She tried to blink the fog away, but it did nothing.

Something's wrong... She knew it, but her mind could not quite process the information, like there was a vast disconnect between her body and her brain. All she was capable of doing was following Mrs. Chattoway all the way up the stairs, and down a cavernous hallway, to the first room on the right. There, the housekeeper directed her to the large four-poster bed, and helped her to lay down beneath soft woollen blankets.

The moment Ada's head hit the pillow, the world spun around her, forcing her to shut her eyes in the hopes of making the whirlwind vanish. Instead, it only invited in the darkness of oblivion.

Seconds before the shadows claimed her, she was aware of a familiar voice, whispering furtively. His deep tenor grumbled across the room to her ears, but she could not urge her eyes to open again.

"We can start the sale now," said Mr. Beauregard, as Ada lost her grip on consciousness.

Chapter Eight

Fanged monsters and sentient shadows plagued Ada's slumbering mind. Jaws snapped in the darkness of her dreams, where she ran frantically along endless hallways; a nightmare labyrinth with jarring twists and turns that kept her no more than a few paces ahead of the wolves that bayed for her blood.

Did I eat too much? Was the food too rich? She strained to open her eyelids, feeling as though she had been struck with a crate of stone. Her dry mouth begged for water, and her heart hammered in her chest as the room around her came into slow focus. An unfamiliar bedchamber, where she lay on an unfamiliar bed, in a house that was not her own, and where the concept of time no longer made any sense.

"Is the hour so late?" Ada tried to sit up, only for a sharp pain in her skull to send her back down into the smothering embrace of the pillows. Outside the nearest window, she could see no sign of daylight. Sunset must have been and gone, but there was no clock to tell her just how long she had slept.

My brothers... I've got to get to my brothers. She tried to sit up again, pushing through the pain in her head. A wave of nausea swept over her, prompting her to lurch over her crossed legs until it passed.

In that moment of silence, she heard a sound, coming from downstairs. The low, rumbling chatter of men. A lot of them, by the sound of it. Every so often, she heard the pistol-shot bark of a bawdy laugh, mingling with raucous shouts and bringing more harsh laughter with them.

We can start the sale now... The memory of Mr. Beauregard's last words, before she fell asleep, crept back into her throbbing head. Still waiting for the nausea to leave, she wondered what it was that the gentleman was selling. He had many fine items in the house. Perhaps, he was mounting some sort of auction, in order to be rid of some of the pieces he no longer cared for.

Pressing a palm to her temple, she battled with the blankets in an attempt to shuffle to the edge of the bed. Even if the sun had only just set, she knew she had overstayed her welcome. Her brothers would be hungry by now, and they would start to fret if she did not return at a reasonable hour.

"They'll be so happy," she whispered, determined to get up, say her thanks to Mr. Beauregard and Mrs. Chattoway, and be out of this house before the unknown auction began.

But her legs would not cooperate. After putting her two feet on solid ground and using her weakened hands to propel her upward, her knees began to shake violently.

Struggling for balance, her legs could not hold up her weight. Her ankles buckled, sending her tumbling backward onto the bed. She lay there, breathless, her head swimming.

I shouldn't have eaten so much, she lamented, her gaze turned up toward the corniced ceiling.

"I'll just rest a moment until my legs feel stronger," she said softly, as her eyes closed, and her breathing slowed. She had only meant to take a brief reprieve from her efforts, but before she could stop it, sleep claimed her once more. This time, there were no dreams or nightmares, only a deep, still darkness that shrouded her weary bones.

"Miss Blair?" A masculine voice coaxed her out of that warm, comforting bubble.

Her eyes opened slightly. "Hmm?"

"Are you awake?"

She felt the bed give, as if someone had sat down on the edge. "I... don't know. Maybe," she croaked, squinting at the blurry figure. Mr. Beauregard cast her a fuzzy smile, and she thought she felt him take her hand, though nothing seemed quite real to her, at that moment. It might well have been her addled imagination.

"I wanted to talk with you awhile, if you are able?" he said.

"Oh... yes... of course," she murmured, passing out before he could say another word.

Chapter Nine

Glaring noonday sunlight filtered through Ada's lids, urging her awake, like the bronzed flash of a warning beacon. Her mind utterly disoriented, even opening her eyes offered no answers. Beneath her, she felt the soft stuffing of a mattress, while the pillow, and the bedclothes tucked around her, were silky and expensive. Nothing she could ever have afforded.

Where am I? She fought to remember, as her blurred vision began to clear. She appeared to be in a fine bedchamber, where heavy velvet drapes concealed much of the large window. The air around her smelled strange: foetid and thick, as though someone were sick.

Am I sick? She wriggled a hand free of the coverlet and brought it to her forehead, though she could not tell if she felt warmer than usual. Still, her body ached as though she were suffering an affliction, and her stomach roiled with nausea, while her throat begged for water.

Turning over on the bed, she found a glass of water on the bedside table. Pushing back to the bed linen so she could reach it, she froze. These were not her clothes. She did not even own a nightgown, and certainly not one of pure, lavender silk; the kind she had heard much older, richer women wore.

"What is that smell?" She sniffed the air, scenting something beneath the fug of the room. A clean, sweet aroma, like rosewater.

It took several moments for her mind to realize that it was coming from her. Puzzled, she bent closer to her arm and sniffed again. There could be no mistaking it. Her skin was soft and scrubbed clean, as though she had taken a bath, but she could not recall doing so. And when she lifted a hand to her hair, she found it tumbling in loose curls, past her shoulders, as silken and smooth as the rest of her.

"Perhaps, I fell ill after that stew," she thought aloud, for it was the last thing she could remember. "Maybe I was sick on myself, so Mr. Beauregard had that housekeeper give me a bath." It seemed like the likeliest explanation, though she had no evidence to confirm it. When it came to Mr. Beauregard and Mrs. Chattoway, after Ada had finished her supper, her mind was a total blank.

Picking up the glass of water, she drank it down to the dregs, before rolling back onto the bed. It really was very comfortable, and it had been a long while since she had been allowed the luxury of a lengthy sleep. Indeed, she almost closed her eyes and tried to drift back off, when a sharp pain blistered across her abdomen.

An uncomfortable gasp escaped her throat as she tried to rub comforting circles across that painful part of her, the way she did when her monthlies came. At first, she had mistaken the dull stabbing sensation for a stomach-ache, courtesy of the rich food she had eaten last night. But the pain was not in the right place. Nor could it be her monthlies, for they had ended only a few days prior.

Something's wrong... Something's terribly wrong. She sat up in a panic, but it only made the pain worse. And, with it, a new sensation of soreness, in places she had never felt sore before. Almost as though she had been burned, and the heat had not yet begun to cool.

"My brothers!" she hissed, scrabbling for the coverlet and throwing it back. In her confusion, she had forgotten about her dear boys. They would be so worried about her, by now, especially as it appeared she had not returned home. Would they have eaten? Would they have been able to find enough to make dinner for themselves? It broke her heart to think of them going hungry.

Forgive me, boys. I'll be home soon.

However, before she could even force herself to get off the bed, the bedchamber door swung wide and Mrs. Chattoway entered, bearing a breakfast tray.

"I hoped you'd be awake," she said, crossing the room and setting the tray down on a table beside the now-dead ashes of a fireplace. "There's no need to rise, Miss Blair. You should rest for the day. You've had a very tiring evening, and I'm sure you are feeling the effects."

Ada stared at the older woman. "What h-happened? I d-don't remember anything after I ate."

"You entertained our honoured guests at the auction." Mrs. Chattoway poured out a cup of tea and brought it to Ada, who had begun to shake violently. Her body seemed to remember something that her mind still could not.

"Guests? What g-guests?" Ada stammered.

Mrs. Chattoway smiled coldly. "Mr. Beauregard's guests, though he was successful in winning the auction, as he so often is. From what I hear, you were everything he had hoped for."

Realisation struck Ada like a knife to the gut, the icy blade of truth twisting her insides. Now, the odd, painful sensation made sense. Mr. Beauregard, a gentleman whom she had trusted, had raped her.

"The stew..." Ada stared at the older woman, with despair in her eyes. "Y-You put something in the stew."

Mrs. Chattoway tried to offer the cup, but Ada batted it away. "Now, there is no need for rudeness. Indeed, there was something in the stew, but it was put there to aid you, so you would not inadvertently embarrass Mr. Beauregard in front of his guests. It is for the best that you were still and silent."

A fresh wave of nausea churned in Ada's stomach, rising up her throat. "He... stole my honour while I... was asleep." The world span around her, and black spots danced in her field of vision. "I... trusted him, and took... he took..."

"Your virginity, yes," Mrs. Chattoway interjected. "Do not be glum about it, Miss Blair. There are only a select handful who can say they gave their honour to Mr. Beauregard."

Ada burst into terrified tears.

"Come now, I am assured that he is always gentle, which cannot be said for the sort of brutes who reside in your lower-class world."

A sudden, brutal grief surged over her, grief for th something she could never get back. Something she had wanted to give to the man who would be her husband. And now, it had been snatched away from her, as though Mr. Beauregard had come into this bedchamber in the night and gutted her whole, leaving her empty and hollow. No... it was worse than that. It felt as if he had replaced her insides with rotten meat, fouled and decaying.

"I w-want to go h-home now," she sobbed, fighting with the bedclothes that writhed around her bare legs. Serpents come to trap her here. "My brothers are w-waiting. I need to g-get back to them."

Mrs. Chattoway laughed. "Oh, my dear Miss Blair, you have no home to return to. Your home is with me, now."

"No, no, please, Mrs. Chattoway!" Ada's eyes flew wide. "I won't say a word about what's been done to me here. I'll keep my mouth shut. Just let me go back to my brothers! They won't survive without me!"

Mrs. Chattoway shrugged. "That really is none of my concern, Miss Blair. You work for me now, and I am looking forward to seeing how you flourish in my house of exotic birds. You are so young and fresh, and with that vibrant, fiery hair of yours, I imagine you will fetch quite the price." Her eyes glinted with joy, as though she could already feel the coins in her palms.

"A brothel?" Ada hunched over, clenching her hands into fists, like she could will away this nightmare.

"Ah, I see you mistook this house for Mr. Beauregard's home. No, no, this house belongs to me." Mrs. Chattoway snorted. "You should be thrilled that the auction was a success, instead of ranting and raving in so ungrateful a manner. As I have already said, Mr. Beauregard seems to be very happy with your participation."

Ada glowered at the woman. "I didn't participate! I was defiled!"

"To the gentlemen who pay so very well for the privilege, they are one and the same," Mrs. Chattoway shot back. "And my master is paid extremely well for procuring beautiful virgins, such as yourself, who will not spread any ailment to his guests. Even though he does use some of that payment to have his own enjoyment, from time to time. He must be truly fond of you, if he won the auction on your behalf."

Ada tried to stand up, but Mrs. Chattoway pushed her back down. "I don't want his fondness, if this is how he shows it!" Ada screamed. "I don't want to be here, and I don't want to work in your brothel, you viper!"

"Unfortunately, you have already been bought, so you have no say in the matter," the older woman said coolly. "But, as most of my girls do, you will get used to the work in due course. Some even come to like it."

Ada tasted the salt of her tears in her mouth. "Then kill me. I'd rather be dead than work in a brothel, selling myself." She gripped the bedclothes. "I mean it, Mrs. Chattoway. Kill me. I won't do as you ask."

The housekeeper smirked. "They all say that, but it changes nothing. It is done. Get used to it."

Turning on her heel, the older woman left the bedchamber, and Ada heard the sound of a key turning in the lock, trapping her within.

"Just let me go home," Ada sobbed into her hands, knowing that no-one would hear, and no-one would care. "Please... just let me go home to my brothers."

But there was no cavalry to come to her rescue, and as her eyes began to blur once more, and her head felt fuzzy, she realised that the water on the bedside table had not been a kindness. It had been a contingency, in case she tried to fight. Soon, she would return to unconsciousness, the choice out of her control.

And tonight, she realised, *I'm going to be sold again.*

Chapter Ten

Months went by in a nightmarish haze beyond Ada's control. When she fought for her freedom, she was rewarded with a pungent tonic, forced down her neck to make her sleep. When she did not fight, sometimes the vermin who came to claim her body asked that she might be rendered unconscious anyway. These men of vile and vulgar tastes were as singular in their likes as in their personalities: some liked their prey listless, some screaming, some fighting tooth and nail, while others made rather twisted attempts at chivalry or kindness, though it all ended the same way.

Ada had played every part and despised them with equal disgust. One might think unconsciousness was the kindest, but she knew better. Awaking to an aching body, mysterious bruises, and deep pains, she could only imagine what the client had done to her. And her imagination was often her worst enemy, making her crave more of the pungent tonic so she would not have to think of the violations that had been wrought upon her.

It's no use... I'll never get out of this place. She sat beside the door to her chamber; the same one she had first been brought to, after eating that ill-fated stew.

Despite the passage of time, it did not stop her from trying to pick the lock on the door every time she was awake and alert, and not languishing in a stupor from whatever Mrs. Chattoway had forced upon her the night before.

"You should stop," a voice whispered through the keyhole, taking Ada by surprise. In three months, nobody had ever spoken to her, aside from Mrs. Chattoway and Mr. Beauregard, on the evenings when he came to satisfy himself at Ada's expense. His prize filly, whom he had wrangled from the streets.

"Is... someone out there?" Ada replied, feeling foolish.

Of course there was someone out there. She had just heard them. But, on occasion, her mind like to play tricks on her, especially when the tonic was wearing off.

So many days, she would imagine she saw her brothers sitting by the fireplace in her bedchamber or running amok in the gardens outside her fancy prison.

But the truth was, she did not know where they were, or what had happened to them. Outside news was not permitted, no matter how she begged.

"Violet Kent," the voice announced, her accent as common as Ada's. "You must be Ada Blair—the hidden secret everyone keeps talkin' about."

Ada's heart leapt. "Can you let me out? Do you have the key?"

"Aye, an' get me arse whipped by Chattoway's cane. No ta."

The woman snorted. "Take it from a girl who knows, Ada, ye're best off just learnin' to enjoy it. I were like you when I first came here—cryin' all the time and beggin' to be let go, but it don't do anyone no good."

"Please..." Ada's breath hitched. "I can't be here. I need to get out. I need to go home."

Violet laughed coldly. "This is your home, 'til you're too old to be worth aught."

"Then... bring me something I can use to... end this," Ada begged, tears prickling her eyes. No matter what this woman said, she would never learn to 'enjoy' it, nor would she learn to just be still and quiet. If she had no hope of escape, then she would remove herself from the equation, and pray that she met her brothers in the hereafter.

Violet rapped her knuckles on the door. "Ye ought to be grateful for this, Ada. Ye're makin' good money for barely any effort, gettin' fed three meals a day, and livin' in luxury. D'ye think ye'd get that outside? Ye ain't stupid. This is the best someone like us is goin' to get, so count yerself lucky that ye're bein' favoured. So, take my advice: give in and do this willingly, or ye're only makin' trouble for yerself."

"Grateful?" Ada spat, suddenly enraged. "I can't even bathe without Mrs. Chattoway's henchman standing outside the door, sneaking looks at me."

"Then stop tryin' to run away, and they won't put Eddie outside the door no more," Violet retorted.

She waited a moment and said more gently, "He don't get a peek for free, with me nor any of the other girls what do as they're told. Halt yer whinin' and ye might get to see daylight again."

Ada heard the sound of rustling, as though someone were standing up. A moment later, the unmistakeable patter of footsteps receded from the doorway, and Ada realised that she was alone again. Violet had said her piece and gone, and Ada had two choices ahead of her: continue to battle against the inevitable, or surrender to this fate.

"I won't give up," she hissed at the locked door. "I won't give up 'til someone tells me what's happened to my brothers. Even then, I won't stop fighting until I see them again, whether it's in this life or the next."

Chapter Eleven

A prisoner, still innocent in some distant memory, though her body had been corrupted and abused to a husk of its former self, Ada slept and woke, ate a few mouthfuls of whatever had been left on her table, and slept again until night came and the monsters prowled at her door once more. Scraping. Scratching. Growling in their throats, pinning her down until she could not breathe.

But, unlike a prisoner, she had no given sentence, nor a given date when the torment would be over, and she could walk free again.

Six months had been and gone, yet every day had blurred into one, until it felt as though she had been here for a day and a decade, all at once.

Now, when she looked in the mirror, she did not recognise the vacant eyes of the stranger staring back. Her clavicles protruded more than before, and Mrs. Chattoway employed clever fabrics in Ada's nightgowns, to conceal the weight that the girl had lost, and could ill afford to lose.

One afternoon, Ada sat by the window, gazing out at a world she could barely recall. The seasons had changed through the square-hatched, rectangular pane of glass.

She had seen the leaves die, and snow blanket the ground, and now she noted the fresh buds upon the sparse trees in the private garden opposite. The tiny square of park where children played and women walked, oblivious to the hostage who watched them, with hauntingly sad eyes.

Those free people would enjoy the coming spring, but Ada would not. What did it matter to her what the weather was like, or how warm the sun was, when she could not feel it?

"Are you still out there?" Ada whispered; her reservoir of tears drained dry. "Jacob, Joshua... are you still alive? Are you managing? Or... are you gone?"

She hung her head, weighed down by the world of shame and grief and pain upon her. Every day, when Mrs. Chattoway came, she asked for news of her brothers without fail. And that old harpy said the same thing, time and again: "Put them out of your mind, Miss Blair. You have no say in their fate any longer. If they have survived, be glad. If they have not... well, at least they have been spared the hardship of the world they lived in. You ought to be grateful, either way."

But how could she be grateful, knowing that it was her stupidity that might have killed them? If she had not been so trusting, if she had not been drawn in by Mr. Beauregard's kindness, if she had not been so eager for a taste of stew and the promise of taking some to feed the boys, then perhaps they would all still be together.

And you, Elijah... How are you faring" Her teeth grazed her dry, chapped lips. *Do you ever think of me? Do you ever wonder where I went? Did you try to look for me?*

She sagged to the floor and rolled her head in her hands, thinking of her beloved friend. The young man with whom she had envisioned an entire future, when they were old enough to understand their feelings. He was the one she had wanted to kiss her for the very first time. He was the one she had wanted to hold her close. He was the one she had wanted to wake up beside, when they were married and utterly, hopelessly in love, the way she had heard about in fairy stories. No, not fairy stories. That was not real. She had wanted to love Elijah the way her mother and father had loved one another, when he had still lived.

Is this where we end up, we women, when we lose the one we love? After all, her mother was in a brothel somewhere, doing the same thing that Ada was doing. Though, at least her mother had been in possession of some knowledge as to how carnal acts worked. That had been a rather brutal awakening for Ada. Truly, she did not understand how anyone could enjoy it, or desire it. If she had a choice, she would run screaming from the touch of a man and never allow herself to be close to one again.

"When the next snow falls, if I'm still here, I'll make sure I don't survive the winter," she told the cloudless sky, that seemed to taunt her with its azure purity. "I'll smash this window when the wind is coldest, and I'll sit beside it, and I'll let it take me away to a better place."

She had seen the cold weather take enough lives, when her family lived in Hackney and on the Isle of Dogs. Why not hers? If she continued to only eat small amounts, it would not take long for the shivering and the exposure to send her to her grave. And when she reached the Kingdom of Heaven, if the Lord allowed her broken and beaten body through the gates, she would meet again with her father and her brothers. If the latter were not yet there, then she would wait.

But I won't wait for you, Ma. If you'd not left us, none of this would've happened. We'd have had money enough for food, and I wouldn't have had to follow a man like Mr. Beauregard to fill my brothers' stomachs.

Suddenly, she heard the key turn in the lock of her bedchamber. Her head snapped up in surprise, for she had already received her luncheon and had it removed, and Mrs. Chattoway never visited outside the times for Ada's meals or her daily bathing.

"No, no, no, no..." Ada began to panic, fearing it might be an afternoon caller. She did not have to contend with them often, but she was always awake and aware when they did. And she was in no mind or mood to have to suffer through abuse right now, with all of her faculties intact.

Her heart sank even further as she witnessed Mr. Beauregard stepping into the room, taking care to lock it behind him so she could not escape. In the past six months, she had become well known for trying to run past anyone who opened the door. This had been a tragic exception, for she had become so used to the routine of the day, that she had not expected someone to enter before evening fell. She had lowered her guard and missed a vital opportunity.

"My dove, why are you hiding underneath the sill?" Mr. Beauregard asked, with no sense of guilt for what he had done to her. "Come here to me."

Ada glared at him instead. "I won't."

"You cannot still be cross with me." He gave a slight chuckle. "You have become the rarest bird in all of London. I cannot go to any gentleman's club without hearing of you and your delight. I must say, it has made me rather jealous."

"Where are my brothers?" she hissed, like a wild animal, cornered by a predator.

Mr. Beauregard frowned. "I do not know, as I have told you on countless occasions. I imagine they are faring well, wherever they may be. Street urchins have a rather excellent habit of enduring almost anything."

No... we can break. You'd know that if you bothered to think of me as a person instead of a piece of meat that you bought and sold.

"What do you want?" Ada turned her gaze away from him. Of course, she had an idea of what he wanted, if he was visiting her in the middle of the afternoon, but she wanted to hear him say it. She wanted him to have to speak his crime aloud.

He took a step towards her. "As I mentioned, all of this talk about you at the club has made me somewhat jealous. For that reason, I have decided to purchase you from this house, and you will be coming with me this very afternoon, to live at my personal residence."

He moved nearer. "You are to be my mistress, Miss Blair. The documents have already been signed. I assure you, I will pay you well for your time with me, and you can expect the finest garments and jewellery to bedeck yourself, as well as anything else you might care for."

Ada's eyes snapped back to him. "And what if the only thing I care about is my freedom?"

Mr. Beauregard's expression hardened. "Miss Blair, you can come with me willingly, or Mrs. Chattoway will give you a dose of her tonic, and you will be carried out of here that way." He gestured to the bedchamber door. "I will have bottles of the same tonic at my residence, should you decide to be... difficult. But I put this to you, Miss Blair: would you rather be permitted to wander through my house as you please, or be locked in the bedroom until your youth and beauty has faded?"

"How can I be sure you won't lock me in the bedchamber, anyway?" Ada shot back.

He smiled. "I will be taking precautions, but I would rather you felt freer in my household than be forced to remain in this paltry room forever."

So, he'll have people watching me, and he'll keep the front door locked. He was merely offering a larger cage for her to prowl around. And yet, she was no fool. She might have missed her opportunity to push past him and flee, but she could not continue here, as she was.

I'm already ruined... At least I'll only have to endure one man, instead of whoever walks through that door, taking a fancy to me each night.

Not only that, but if she had a hint of freedom, maybe she would be able to find her moment to wriggle off his hook and escape. She would certainly have more hope in a house where she had freer rein, than stuck in this bedchamber.

Holding his gaze, she tried not to smile, lest she give her thoughts away. "How can I say no to that?

Chapter Twelve

It should have been a joyous moment for Ada, when she stepped out of Mrs. Chattoway's bawdy house for the first time in six months. To feel the sunlight on her pale face, and the kiss of a breeze upon her cheeks, and to hear the birdsong of blackbirds trilling in the nearby branches. Instead, the sensations and noises struck her in an overwhelming wave: too loud, too brash, too bright. It was as though she had forgotten how to be a part of this world.

"If you please, Miss Blair." Mr. Beauregard directed her towards a waiting carriage. There would be no luggage accompanying her, for the nightgowns and dresses she had worn within the townhouse belonged to Mrs. Chattoway. Nor would Ada have wanted to take them with her, considering the bitter memories in every silken thread.

Ada's sun-blinded eyes darted left and right, knowing this was her chance run. She was outside. There were people wandering the streets. All she had to do was sprint away and call to someone for help, and perhaps this nightmare would come to an end.

Apparently sensing her intent, Mr. Beauregard seized her by the wrist. "Remember what we discussed. If you behave poorly, you will be gagged and bound, and you will not be allowed any freedom when we reach my residence. Run, and you will regret it."

"I wasn't planning to," she lied, as he all but dragged her to the carriage and shoved her inside before she could cause a scene.

Once the carriage door closed behind her, she knew she had missed another opportunity. And yet, considering her malnourished state, and the lack of exercise her legs had received over the last half a year, she was not even sure that they would have been able to run fast enough to escape Mr. Beauregard, or Mrs. Chattoway's guards, who stood on the steps, overseeing Ada's departure.

Just then, the vicious woman herself came to the window, and smiled up at Ada as though nothing bad had occurred between them. "You see, Miss Blair. I assured you that you would be well taken care of, and now you are to be the mistress of one of London's finest gentlemen. I must say, despite all of your protestations, you have served me exceptionally well. I cannot remember a time when my coffers were so full, though there will be so much disappointment when it is discovered that you have been bought."

"I'm sure you'll just take another hapless girl off the streets, to take my place," Ada spat back, already feeling sorry for the young, naïve creature who did not yet know what might befall her.

Mrs. Chattoway laughed. "One can only hope, Miss Blair."

With that, Mr. Beauregard instructed the driver to move off, and the carriage took Ada away from the brothel, to whatever lay in store for her new position as mistress.

Ada leaned against the side of the carriage, trying to put as much distance between herself and Mr. Beauregard as possible, while she turned her gaze to the passing scenery of London's more affluent locales. She stared at the passers-by, wondering if they knew what was going under their noses, wondering if they cared. She supposed, if it did not directly affect them, then why should they concern themselves with the plight of a lowly woman who had come from nothing?

So, it came as something of a surprise when the carriage came to a halt barely five streets away from the brothel she had just left.

"Do you have an errand to run?" Ada asked, for that was the only reason she could think of for this sudden stop.

Mr. Beauregard shook his head. "No, Miss Blair. This is your new home." He opened the carriage door and stepped out, before offering his hand to her.

Reluctantly, she took it, and alighted from the darkened carriage interior. A grand, sandstone townhouse stood ahead of her. Much nicer than the brothel, yet not quite as architecturally awe-inspiring as the Mayfair townhouses that she had occasionally passed whilst scouring the streets for cigar ends.

"But... it's so close to Mrs. Chattoway's house," Ada said in disbelief. "Why did you bring a carriage when we could've walked?"

He gave her a pointed look. "I believe you already know the answer to that, Miss Blair."

Because I would've run...

"Now, if you would follow me." He seized her by the wrist once more and led her up the marbled porch steps to his residence.

Once inside, she was barely given the opportunity to take in her new surroundings. A cavernous entrance hall greeted her coldly, whilst blank-eyed statues and painted spectators seemed to watch her every movement as she was taken up the curved staircase to the upper floor.

Mr. Beauregard did not let go of her wrist until they reached the last door at the very end of a long hallway; the only door that could be plainly seen from the top of the stairwell. Ada supposed that was no coincidence. He wanted his household to notice whenever she came in and out of her soon-to-be bedchamber.

Taking out a key, he slipped it in the lock. "This will be your new abode. I shall leave you in here for a while, to become better acquainted with the room, and with the garments that I have selected for you. In an hour, I shall send your new lady's maid to dress you for the evening."

Ada frowned. "Why, what's happening this evening?"

As if I don't already know...

He smiled. "I thought it might be pleasant to have a gathering, in honour of your new place here, at my side. And I cannot resist an opportunity to gloat to the other gentlemen, that I have managed to acquire you, and they have not."

Ada felt her muscles tighten with alarm. "Men are... coming to the house?"

"Fear not." He lifted his hand and caressed her cheek, making her freeze. "They will not be permitted to touch you. They may only admire, from afar, what they can never have again."

Her breath quickened in fright as she thought of all the warped faces she had witnessed, looming above her. All the hands pawing at her, all the slimy lips smearing her skin, and the stench of their hot breath upon her. Were they the 'gentlemen' she would have to face again tonight? Would they ogle her and smirk, remembering all they had done to her? She might have been taken away from the brothel, but it seemed she could not escape it entirely.

"Would you care for an aperitif, Miss Blair? I imagine it will help you to be more amenable when my guests arrive." It did not sound like a suggestion. It was a command. But Ada had learned not to trust anything she was served by the likes of him.

She forced a smile. "Port or sherry, if you have it."

"Certainly, my dove." He dipped his head and planted a kiss upon her lips, though if he thought she would reciprocate, he was sorely mistaken. Indeed, it took all of her willpower not to bite his horrid, slug-like lips until he bled.

Pulling away, he gave her a slight nudge in the small of the back to get her to cross the threshold into her new bedchamber, before he closed the door behind her. She waited for the usual sound of the key turning, but it did not come.

Evidently, Mr. Beauregard intended to stay true to his word of giving her more liberty in this household, as long as she toed the line.

I just have to lure him into a false sense of security, she told herself. *Once he trusts that I won't run... that's exactly when I'll make my escape.*

Until then, however, she would have to play the role she had been brought here to enact. And, as she looked at the large, luxurious four-poster bed, draped in gauzy fabric, her heart sank like a stone. He would come for her each night. He would be the only monster scratching at her door. But the person who had first said, "better the devil you know," had clearly never been in her position. Sometimes, the devil you knew was far worse than the devil you did not.

~ ~ ~ ~ ~

A brisk Spring transformed into the smouldering heat of Summer, and Ada had submitted to her existence as Mr. Beauregard's mistress. She dressed in the expensive garments of silk and satin that he purchased for her, and wore the fine jewels that he had acquired on her behalf. She accompanied him to the theatre, and served tea to his friends, or acted the beautiful, enigmatic hostess at the parties he held at his house. And she did it all with the same rehearsed, sweet smile, so that her keeper would not suspect the boiling hatred that bubbled in her breast.

"Miss Blair, might I trouble you for another glass of that delicious French brandy?" Mr. Beauregard's acquaintance, a Viscount of some kind, called to her.

She laughed coquettishly. "I believe they call it cognac, dear Viscount." She always altered her accent when in company, smoothing out the roughened edges, as Mr. Beauregard had requested, so that her voice would fit her attire and her jewellery.

"Aha! A learned vixen indeed!" the Viscount cheered, to the delight of the five other gentlemen who had come to carouse and imbibe at Mr. Beauregard's expense.

Ada picked up the decanter of brandy and made sure to lean over the Viscount's shoulder in a tantalising manner, as she poured him a fresh glass. "To your good health, Viscount."

"And to yours, darling Miss Blair." The Viscount licked his lips, eyeing her ravenously. Of all the men in this room, he was the only one she could not recall visiting Mrs. Chattoway's house of ill repute, though she supposed he had heard everything there was to know about her.

"I do believe your eyes shall fall out of your head if you continue to stare at Miss Blair in so intent a manner," another of the gentlemen quipped. A Mr. Dempsey, who had visited her at the brothel on at least two occasions. He had been the sort to attempt chivalry and charm, believing himself a romantic when, in truth, he was just as much a brute as the rest of them.

Mr. Beauregard chuckled. "She is a divine creature."

"I wish Mrs. Chattoway had informed me that Miss Blair was available as a mistress. I might have acquired her for myself," Mr. Dempsey said with a smile.

"Gentlemen, you should not quarrel over a shy young lady like myself. I am certain there is plenty of entertainment to be found, despite my departure, at Mrs. Chattoway's menagerie." Ada fluttered her eyelashes, wishing she could hurl the decanter of brandy over the lot of them, and set this household ablaze. She did not even care if she got caught in the inferno. After three months of being Mr. Beauregard's mistress, it would have been a kindness.

The Viscount sighed. "But those ladies are not nearly as entrancing as you."

"You flatter me." Ada giggled, resenting the sound. "Mr. Beauregard, would you care for more cognac?"

He smiled back at her, clearly pleased by her attention. "Why, yes, that would be most delightful."

She sauntered over to him, in her flowing gown of red silk, with a ruby choker around her neck that threatened to heed its namesake, and poured a large measure into his glass. It was a trick she had learned over the last three months. If she offered him more liquor in front of his guests, he rarely refused, and when he became utterly inebriated, he never came to disturb her in her bedchamber.

Drink your fill, Mr. Beauregard, so I can sleep easily without worrying about you forcing your way into my bed.

She flashed him a winning smile that she had perfected in her looking glass and moved to fill the glasses of the other gentlemen. After a few more hours of pouring cognac, they would all be fast asleep in this drawing room, leaving her to spend her nights at her leisure.

Those were the nights she prayed for, and yet they were less frequent than she would have liked.

There's a price on these fine garments and lavish jewels... and I pay it with my body, whether I want to wear these gaudy trinkets or not.

Turning her back on the gathering to replace the decanter, she stole a secret moment for herself, drawing in steadying breaths. All the while, she felt the eyes of the men upon her, violating her with their stares.

I hate you, Ma. I hate you for running away and leaving me to this fate. I hate you for abandoning my brothers, and making me abandon them, too. You chose this life. I didn't. If I live to be a hundred, I'll never forgive you.

She twirled around to face the gentlemen, touching the choker at her throat. "Who would like to hear a joke?"

A chorus of eager assent rippled back.

My life... my life is the joke.

Chapter Thirteen

The world turned steadily through month after month, until Summer returned to London once more. A whole year under Mr. Beauregard's rule, and Ada had slowly accepted that she would never get out of this house. There had been many a moment where a chance had presented itself, only to be thwarted by the appearance of a henchman at the front door, or waiting on the step outside to catch her if she tried to leave.

Indeed, her only time outside the townhouse were the gilded occasions in which Mr. Beauregard took her to parties, or the theatre, or to dinners and gatherings at the households of his friends. And though she resented admitting it, she rather looked forward to those brief reprieves from her larger prison.

"What do you intend to do today, Miss Blair?" asked Lucinda, her appointed lady's maid. "There's that magnolia muslin in the armoire that you've not worn for an age. Perfect weather for it. We could sit in the garden awhile, take a picnic luncheon out there if the mood takes you?"

Ada smiled at the young woman, who could not have been more than a few years older than her. "I think that sounds rather pleasant." In truth, Ada was in a far better state of mind, thanks to Mr. Beauregard's recent absence from her bedchamber. He had not visited her for a fortnight, which was the longest he had spent away from her since he had brought her here. It certainly made her imprisonment easier to bear, when she did not have to contend with the additional punishment of his so-called affections.

"I'll have to find your parasol. You know how Mr. Beauregard hates it when you get freckles," Lucinda said, humming to herself as she sifted through the armoire of garments, looking for the magnolia muslin.

"It's nice to have a garden," Ada thought aloud, as she perched up on the sill and glanced out at the emerald lawns, bordered by vibrant wildflowers. Bumblebees thrummed from bloom to bloom, collecting their pollen on their adorable, furred bodies. She knew many young ladies who were terrified of bumblebees, but she could never be afraid of something so sweet and industrious. In a way, they reminded her of her lost sister, who had always buzzed hither and thither, gathering treasure from the mud.

Lucinda took out the dress. "Oh, I'm sure you're glad of it in this heat." She paused and lowered her voice. "One of these days, you should ask Mr. Beauregard for permission to go and walk in Hyde Park, and take me with you!"

"I will do my best." Ada chuckled, her heart lighter than it had been in more than two years, since her mother abandoned her family.

She still thought of her brothers often, and hoped they were well somewhere, but she had come to understand that there was nothing she could do about her situation. Or theirs. Not whilst Mr. Beauregard remained her keeper.

"I've heard the most handsome gentlemen in London ride the pathways of Hyde Park on their majestic horses. I bet they would tip their hats to you, Miss Blair!" Lucinda enthused giddily, but Ada shook her head.

"I wouldn't want their attention, Lucinda. If a man never looks at me again, it'll be too soon," she said quietly. "I know too much about what goes on inside their minds to ever trust a man again."

Unless it was you, Elijah. I could trust you, though what good would it do? I'm ruined. I'm despoiled. Even if you could look past that, I don't know that I'd ever be able to let you get close to me.

Besides, she knew he had likely forgotten her by now. After nearly two years as a prisoner in Mrs. Chattoway's brothel and Mr. Beauregard's house, he had probably assumed she was dead. In a way, he would not be wrong, for the Ada he had known no longer existed. She had died the first night that Mr. Beauregard had stolen her honour from her.

"Do you want to wear the pearls with this, Miss Blair?" Lucina brought the garment over and rested it against Ada, assessing the pastel shade against her skin.

Ada smoothed a hand across the fabric. "No, I don't think I'll wear any jewellery today."

"But Mr. Beauregard likes it when you wear the jewels he's bought you," Lucinda protested.

Ada flashed her a smile. "Precisely."

"Miss, you shouldn't rile him up. It's easier for you when you do what he wants." Lucinda looked anxious, for though the two women had become close over the past year, Ada knew that her lady's maid always obeyed Mr. Beauregard's wishes first, and Ada's second.

Ada shrugged. "I don't want anything strangling my neck whilst I'm enjoying an afternoon in the garden."

"I suppose Mr. Beauregard doesn't have to see you. He's been away from the house a lot, lately. As long as I put a necklace on you by this evening, I'm sure everything will be well." Seemingly appeased, Lucinda began to help Ada dress.

It was a part of her life that Ada would never get used to. Until she was taken to the brothel, she had always dressed and undressed herself. Sometimes, she tried to insist that Lucinda let her do it by herself, but the lady's maid always refused. Ada supposed the slightly older woman did not understand that she did not like to be touched, and she did not want to upset the only person who had come close to being a friend. As such, she endured it as best she could, trying not to flinch whenever Lucinda's fingertips grazed her skin accidentally.

A short while later, dressed in the magnolia-toned muslin, with a yellow ribbon to accentuate her now-shapely figure, Ada and Lucinda were preparing to head out of the bedchamber. They had almost reached the door when it swung open of its own accord, to reveal Mr. Beauregard standing on the threshold.

"Miss Blair... ah, I hope I have not interrupted. I must speak with you." He gave a sharp look to Lucinda, dismissing her without a word. The lady's maid curtsied hurriedly and exited the room, taking Ada's last line of defence with her.

"What did you want to say to me?" Ada replied coolly, scrutinising him. "It seems urgent."

He folded his hands behind his back. "Indeed, it is."

"Then don't leave me in suspense." In return, she folded her arms across her chest. There was something about his general demeanour that had her on tenterhooks. For one thing, he had never missed an opportunity to yank her into his arms, and yet he was maintaining a polite distance.

Like you did when we first met, you cretin.

"Miss Blair, you have been with me for a year now, and I have not regretted a moment of installing you here as my mistress. However..." He paused with a sigh. "However, I have unfortunately grown tired of your particular charms. Though do not be disheartened, Miss Blair, for you have been my mistress far longer than any of the ladies who have come before."

Ada stared at him. "You're... getting rid of me?"

"Replacing you might be a fairer term, for a younger creature has rather caught my eye, and you must depart if I am to bring her here," he continued, as though he were merely informing her that he wished to change the drapes in her bedchamber. "It has been a pleasure, Miss Blair." He put out his hand for her to shake, but she did not move.

"Does this mean... I'm free?"

Her head swam with countless thoughts, and yet his delivery was so blunt that she could not begin to fathom that this might be real. That, after almost two years of incarceration, she would be allowed to walk from this house without anyone stopping her.

He nodded. "It does, Miss Blair." Retracting his handshake, he dipped into his pocket and produced a velvet pouch, heavy with coin. "This is your compensation, for the time we have spent together. And you may wear and keep this dress, or another from your wardrobe, though the rest will remain in my possession."

"Can I leave *now*?" She took the pouch of money and thought of the jewellery box on her vanity. If she could take just one necklace, it would gain her a generous sum when she sold it, to outlast the coin he had given her.

He smiled, as though reading her mind. "I will know if you steal one of the jewellery pieces, so do not even contemplate it. The money in that purse is ample recompense, and I imagine the muslin of your dress will fetch a decent sum, should you run short."

"Then... I'll take a cloak and leave immediately." She did not want to hesitate, in case he changed his mind.

"Very well." He waited as she ran to the wardrobe and took out a cloak of dark, navy wool and clutched it to her chest.

She would not need it now, whilst the summer was fearsomely hot, but she would thank herself for taking it when winter came.

With all her worldly possession diminished to one pouch of coins, the clothes on her back and bundled into her arms, and the boots upon her feet, she fled from the bedchamber without so much as a goodbye. It was not as though they were ardent lovers, bidding each other a fond and heart-breaking farewell.

Reaching the entrance hall, she slowed to a tentative shuffle on her approach to the front door, fearing it might be a cruel trick of some kind. But Mr. Beauregard's two stoic henchmen merely dipped their heads to her, with one even opening the door so she could leave without delay.

As she stepped out into the molasses-thick air, and walked down to the level of the street, she paused and leaned up against the balustrade of the porch. This was the dream she had longed for, even in the darkest pits of her despair. Her sentence was finally over, and she could walk as a free woman once again.

She could go anywhere without anyone grabbing her and dragging her back to her bedchamber. Indeed, she could finally venture out into the city and, God willing, find the beloved brothers who had likely given up hope of her ever returning.

Please be alive, she prayed silently. *Please... please be alive.*

Standing there, raking in harsh breaths, she felt a warm tear roll down her cheek. Before she knew it, she was crouched low in front of the house, weeping until her throat felt raw and her eyes stung with the salt of her grief. There, she shed the tears of a woman who had survived everything the world could throw at her, and the tears of the young girl whose innocence had been lost within the walls of two strange houses.

She did not know which was sadder, but it did not matter. Finally, she was allowed to let go of everything that had been building within her, all this time.

The tears might never have stopped, had it not been for the sound of carriage wheels rattling in her direction.

Ada lifted her head and rubbed her eyes clear of the blur, as the carriage came to a stop beside her and a face appeared at the window. A face she did not want to see, ever again.

"My dear girl, I hoped I might find you here," Mrs. Chattoway said with saccharine sweetness. "Mr. Beauregard informed me that he wished to dispense with you, so I thought I would come to you, and say that you can return to work at my menagerie now."

Ada's eyes narrowed. "Not if you paid me all the money in Christendom."

"I still own you, Miss Blair." Mrs. Chattoway's pleasant mask slipped, revealing the snake beneath. "It was not a request."

Ada smiled coldly. "I don't belong to anyone but myself."

She jumped up to her full height, as the carriage door burst open and Mrs. Chattoway attempted to lunge for her. Ada feinted to the side, missing the old woman's snatching hand by a hair's breadth, and took off down the street as fast as her legs would carry her. Taking no risks, she darted down every side street and narrow alleyway that she could find, making sure she was sprinting down a path that no carriage could follow.

"I'm free," she whispered, heart pounding. "I'm finally free."

Chapter Fourteen

Roaming the streets of London for the next few days, Ada kept one eye over her shoulder, terrified that Mrs. Chattoway might appear from the shadows and ensnare her once again. It did not matter that Mr. Beauregard had deemed her too old for his purposes, for she knew that she was still profitable in the eyes of someone like that wretched old witch.

But she had coin in her purse, and a dress that had already added to her meagre fortune, for she had sold it within hours of leaving Mr. Beauregard's house, and had used a small portion of it to buy a more suitable dress. After all, the last thing she wanted was to get robbed upon the streets because she looked too fine in expensive garments.

"Good morning to you," she said to the hunched crone on the stairwell of her new lodgings in Shadwell. The cheapest room she had been able to find, without having to share. For, if she was going to find her brothers, she wanted to have a place ready for them to live in.

The woman scowled at her. "What's so good about it, eh?"

"Uh... nothing. Sorry." Ada hurried on her way, determined to find employment before the day was done. It was her third day of searching for work, since her unexpected liberation, and the endeavour had not been as easy as she might have hoped. Apparently, no-one was eager to employ a young lady who did not seem to have any sort of skill.

I'll find work, then I'll find my brothers. If I can't find them on my own, I'll go to Elijah.

In truth, she felt somewhat uneasy about visiting her old friend again. All of the remaining hopes and dreams she had possessed, where he was concerned, had been violated and tormented out of her by Mr. Beauregard's nightly attentions. Even though she knew Elijah to be a good man, she did not feel as though she could face him, having been brought so low.

Discreetly, she patted the secret pocket that she had sewn into the lining of her simple cotton dress. The coins that Mr. Beauregard had given her were not vast, but they would prevent her from starving for a while. She was not foolish enough to leave the velvet pouch in her lodgings, lest someone find it. No, it was far safer to carry it with her, for if any thief so much as touched her, she would not hesitate to scratch their eyes out.

Outside, the cheerful sunlight no longer seemed to goad her, as it had during her imprisonment. She could walk where she pleased and feel its gentle warmth upon her face, and listen to the raucous chatter of London as she went, grateful to be free.

Of course, the streets were still mired in filth, and there were prostitutes, loafers, drunks, and beggars on every corner, but she would not have exchanged her surroundings for the world.

Upon reaching the docks, she strolled along and paused by every stall she saw.

"Are you looking for workers? I can sell fish, and I can gut them, too," she said, repeating the same words after every sour-faced refusal. "Or I can wheel the cart around. Anything you like."

"You'd be better off in a brothel, lass, with a face like yours!" one woman cackled in reply, making Ada's cheeks burn.

She fared little better in the taverns, prompting her to move further inland. There, she stopped by every market stall, every sewing house, every place that she could possibly think of, only to be turned away with the same curt replies:

"You think I haven't already got me hands full with young girls who never stick around?" retorted the sewing house overseer.

"Aye, as if them dainty hands have seen a day's hard labour in their life," snarled the mill owner.

"Me lads wouldn't get a snip of work done, looking at you all the day long," muttered the warehouse supervisor, with a pointed jab at Ada's face.

"You want to work, then scrape a living, like the rest of us!" barked the puckered mouth of a rag and bone man, wheeling his cart away before Ada could beg for a chance.

More despondent than when she had begun, she traipsed the labyrinth of London on weary feet, picking up the odd cigar end and length of ribbon that had been discarded by careless hands. She did not want to return to her old life, exactly as it had been, but perhaps the city was telling her that she had no choice. If she wanted to earn coin for herself, then she would have to do whatever it took, even if that meant scouring and scrounging, as she had done two years prior.

Maybe, she could even return to mudlarking. She had been good at that, and those brutes from the Isle of Dogs would not know her now. Even if they did, she could find a different spot, on this side of the Thames, as far away from them as possible.

"At least I'm not in there," she muttered, as her eyes fell upon the grim, black exterior of a nearby workhouse. Throughout her reasonably short life, she had vowed that she would never be so downtrodden that she would walk through those gates and beg a place amongst the lowest of the low. It was not their fault, and she did not blame those who sought the protection of the workhouse, but she would not allow herself to be one of them.

Quickening her pace to get away from the ominous presence of the workhouse, she found herself walking in the direction of the stonemasonry where Elijah worked with his father. She had not intended to follow such a path, but she could not stop herself. Indeed, her body seemed to know the way better than her mind, for she could not quite recall the way.

She could not have been more than six streets from the door of that stonemasonry workshop, when she jolted backward so suddenly that she felt her neck crack.

At first, she thought she had lost her footing, as she tumbled backward. And then she saw them. Three men, leering at her from the darkness of the alleyway to her right. Above her, a fourth man, with the scruff of her collar clenched in his fist.

She opened her mouth to scream, when another of the lurking wretches lunged out and clamped a hand over her lips, silencing her. Meanwhile, the one who held her hostage by the fabric of her dress tugged her sharply into the gaping void of the alley mouth. The remaining two wasted no time clawing at her arms, dragging her further into the alleyway, where no-one would see the danger she was in.

Thinking quickly, she bit down hard on the second man's hand. He snapped his fingers back as though he had been stung, yelping as he saw a trickle of blood dripping to the ground.

"Get off me!" Ada roared, praying some kind Samaritan would hear, and come to her aid.

"The wench bit me!" the wounded party complained, whilst his accomplices laughed and continued to haul Ada into the terrible depths.

"Serves ye right for puttin' yer hand in the way of her mouth then, eh?" one retorted.

Another grinned. "She won't be wailin' for long, once we're done with her."

"Just to make sure." A third removed the neckerchief from around his throat and knelt on Ada's chest so she could not breathe. As she gasped for air, he shoved the neckerchief into her mouth, forcing her throat to seize up as it tried to draw air past that blockage.

"Let's make this hasty, lads." The bitten man sneered down at her. "Who's going first, eh?"

The one who had dragged her into the alleyway finally let go of her collar. "I think it should be me, since I did the hard work."

"Get on with it, then!" the third man muttered, gesturing at Ada with a filthy hand. "Else the Peelers will be here before we've all had our turn."

At the sound of that threat, and the prospect of what they intended to do, Ada began to fight with everything she had. Her arms flailed wildly and she kicked out with her legs, snarling through the neckerchief like a frightened animal who had no intention of being captured.

The ringleader glanced at his acquaintances with shifty, dark eyes. "Well, hold her down. I'm not gettin' me eyes scratched out."

Just like that, the four men set upon her. One held her legs down with their full bodyweight as she struggled to keep writhing and kicking, whilst the other two gripped an arm each, her bare skin being cut to ribbons by the sharp shards of glass and stone that littered the alley floor. Through the fabric of her dress, she could already feel the dampness of whatever putrid liquid had gathered between the cobbles, but she would rather have bathed in effluence than have these men rape her. Had she not been violated enough?

With a smirk, the ringleader began to tear at her dress, ripping the fabric up the seams. She jerked as her bare legs were exposed to the cold stone, and rolled her body violently from side to side, to try and avoid his unwanted touch.

As he wrenched the waistline of her garment, she froze at the sound of metal clinking to the ground.

No... my purse! It's all I have! Her eyes turned down, watching in horror as her worldly wealth, however paltry, skittered across the alley, the coins rolling like cartwheels until the fell over with a quiet chink.

However, it seemed the men were equally enamoured with the prospect of coin for their own pockets. No sooner had the money liberated itself from Ada's coin pouch than the wretched crooks were all up on their feet, chasing after it. They scrambled like rats scurrying for scraps, releasing Ada from their vice-like clutches.

In that moment, she had to decide: to fight for her life or fight for the coin in that pouch. It was not much of a choice. Moving quickly, she leapt up to her feet and sprinted with all her might down the alleyway, darting past one of the wretches who had stooped to collect coins closer to the entrance. He made a half hearted attempt to grab at her leg, but she sailed over his reach, and barrelled out onto the street.

I have to run... and I have to run as far and as fast as I can. With the remnants of her torn dress flapping around her, revealing the cotton of the pantalettes she had kept from Mr. Beauregard's house as an extra layer, she did not stop fleeing until she found herself back at the docks.

"Have ye seen the state of her?" she heard a cluster of women whisper, but she did not care. They did not know what she had escaped, nor what she had given in order to escape it.

Panting hard, she braced her hands against an iron railing, and stared out at the murky Thames.

Part of her wondered if it might be easier to go to Tower Bridge and simply throw herself into the mercy of the river, for with her sudden pause came a realisation: she could not return to her lodgings. The landlord would throw her out that very same day, now that she had no money to pay the rents, which she was supposed to pay on a nightly basis.

Instead, she began to laugh. A mad, hysterical laugh that could have been mistaken for the howling cry of a wounded animal. People stared and pointed, but she did not see them, or hear them. She heard only the sound of a woman who could not take any more from this wretched city. Those disgusting rats had stolen her last options from her. Now, she had no place to sleep, nothing to fill her gnawing belly, and no place for her brothers, if she found them.

Not only that, but they had robbed her of her chance to go to Elijah, and ask for his help. There was no way she could visit him now, looking as she did. His father would shoo her from the doorway before she could get close.

Go back to Mrs. Chattoway. Beg her to let you back in, her mind taunted, but she refused to listen. If she went back there, she might as well have let those wretches assault her. No, this city could take everything from her, but no-one would have her body again, not for any sum of money.

As her manic laughter died on her lips, she understood the fate before her. The streets she had once scavenged were all she had left, now. And she knew just how cruel and unkind they could be.

Chapter Fifteen

Huddled into the thin protection of a cloak she had fashioned from cloth sacks, as fat, icy snowflakes tumbled from the sky, Ada picked her way through the gloomy early evening of London's bitter winter. After six months on the streets, she had hoped she might become immune to the cold, but the weather was a fickle mistress, and it did so love to torment her.

Her stomach grumbled savagely as she bent to pick up a cigar end, outside a tavern in Soho. They were as rare as rubies in the wintertime, when most enjoyers of cigars took their smoking indoors, but it would be enough to gain her a coin or two. That, in turn, would be enough to grant her the one, thin meal of gruel that she was able to purchase for herself most days.

Suddenly weak on her feet, Ada stumbled to the doorway of a nearby house, and sank down upon the steps. She huddled there with her chin upon her knees, waiting for the dizziness to subside. It had been happening more and more, of late, for she had not been able to supplement her gruel with the scraps and crusts she usually found on her rounds in the warmer months.

With so much snow and rain, the crusts of bread had disintegrated by the time she could get to them, and the vegetable peelings turned to rotten mush in her hands.

I'm going to die out here. I'm going to die, having never found my brothers. They'll never know what happened to their sister. They'll think I left them, like their mother did.

Hunching over, she began to cry, overwhelmed by the emotion that had gathered in her heart over the years since she had been parted from them. For, despite her fatigue and starvation, she had never stopped looking for those beloved boys. She watched the streets for them, and asked anyone who would listen, but no-one could tell her anything. She had even returned to their old lodgings, only to be told that the boys had been cast out not long after she had been taken by Mr. Beauregard.

Maybe it's time I gave up, and I'll just have to hope that I meet them in the hereafter. She might not have given up her search, but she knew the likelihood that they had died long ago, in much the same manner as she felt she was about to. Street urchins had a survival instinct, but they were not invincible, and those boys did not know where to find a meal. She had always seen to that, when their mother could not.

"Miss?" A quiet voice brought her out of her miserable reverie.

Ada lifted her head to find a young boy crouched in front of her. "What is it? Do you want me to move? Is this your spot or something?" She knew she should not speak so harshly to a child, but she was tired to her very bones, and no longer had patience for anything.

"No... I just wanted to give you this." The boy produced a chunk of bread from his pocket and handed it to her, seemingly oblivious to her cold demeanour.

She eyed it. "Why?"

"You look sick, miss. Your bones are sticking out all over. I reckon you need it more than I do," he replied, with a lopsided smile.

Reluctantly, she took the proffered bread and broke off a tiny piece. Putting it into her mouth, she softened it with her saliva first, as her teeth ached from malnourishment and disease. It tasted slightly sweet, as she swallowed it. But she knew it would not be enough to stave off the agony of her hunger, or the ongoing weakness in her limbs. It would only buy her a few more hours, or a few more days, at most.

"You should come to the workhouse where me and me ma live," the boy said, watching her closely. "It ain't pretty, but there's food, and it's not so cold as out here. The work's hard, but at least ye won't be shiverin' and starvin' to death."

She snorted. "How old are you?"

"Nine." The boy beamed, not knowing how much the revelation made her heart ache. Joshua would be nine now, if he was still living.

"What makes you think you're so wise then, if you're only nine?" She held back her tears as she tore off another small piece and softened it on her tongue.

He shrugged. "It's what me ma tells me."

"You're lucky you have a ma that cares," Ada murmured. "If my ma had taken us all to the workhouse, maybe we'd all still be together. Or if she'd just stayed."

"You lost her?" The boy blinked: his face sweet in its childish earnestness.

Ada smiled sadly. "In a way, yes."

"Then come to the workhouse, and me ma can take care of you, an' all." The boy held out a small hand. "It's not far, and I don't think ye'll be alive in the mornin', if ye don't come back with me now. I'm only sayin' that 'cause I walk by here all the time, and I don't want to see ye all frozen and dead when I walk by tomorrow."

Ada narrowed her eyes at him. "Are you sure you're not some sort of angel, about to guide me to heaven?"

He tapped the top of his unruly blonde hair. "Got no halo, Miss. I ain't no angel."

Ada broke off the last piece of bread and popped it into her mouth as she contemplated his suggestion. He was right, in many ways. If she stayed out on the streets, as she had been doing, she would die of exposure or starvation. Whichever got her first.

"I suppose I can't keep going like this," she admitted, more to herself than to him. "And I won't go back to Mrs. Chattoway's house."

"Is that your ma?" the boy asked.

Ada laughed bitterly. "No, she's more what you would call a 'Madam.' But you don't need to know what that means."

The boy nodded. "I already do, and I don't think ye should go back to her, neither. That ain't right for a woman."

"Another pearl of wisdom from your ma?" Ada swallowed the last of the bread.

"Aye."

Hugging her knees, Ada unleashed a heavy sigh. In truth, her life was already over. She had tried to survive on her own terms, and London had thwarted her every move. She had tried to overcome the relentless challenges and had been found wanting. All she could do now was exist for however long she had left, and that meant following this boy to the workhouse, to enter the place she had vowed she would never go.

Gritting her painful teeth, she took the boy's outstretched hand, and allowed him to guide her through the snow-blanketed streets. She did not even shed a tear as she walked through the gates of the workhouse, and through the imposing front doors. After all, this was the last resort of the lowest of the low, and she could not get any lower.

Chapter Sixteen

A few days later, a blizzard hit the city of London in the last gasp of that winter, and though Ada despised the workhouse almost as much as she had despised the streets, she could not deny she felt a sliver of gratitude that she had followed the boy when she had.

His name was Little Stevie, and she would never not be convinced that he was some sort of angel in a filthy, downtrodden disguise.

If he'd found me on those steps a day, or even two days later, I'd be freezing to death with the rest of the poor saps.

Sitting up against the dank, slimy wall of the shadowed corner where she slept, Ada watched the flood of people coming through the doors of the workhouse, only to be turned away by the overseer and his men.

The building was already at capacity and could not take any more of the lowly and hopeless.

It was as good as giving a death sentence.

Surviving a London winter without a roof over one's head could be hard enough on any given year, but with relentless snow falling, and the wind chill unyielding in its ferocity, even the death carts were struggling to collect all of the frozen bodies found in doorways, huddled in alleys, and others where the helpless souls had simply collapsed in the middle of the street.

"I got yer dinner." A face appeared around the rotting wooden partition that separated the former prostitutes from the rest of the populace, like diseased cattle being kept away from the herd.

Ada turned her gaze from the human torrent at the doors. "Does your ma know where you are? I don't want you getting a hiding because of me."

"She don't care," Little Stevie replied nonchalantly, as he sat down on the mouldering blanket that served as Ada's bed, and handed a small bowl of thin gruel to her. Out of his seemingly endless pockets, he produced two stale crusts of bread and added both to Ada's meagre feast.

Ada clicked her tongue. "What are you giving me that for, Stevie? You're a growing lad. I've done all my growing." She pushed the two crusts back into his hands. "I won't eat them with my teeth the way they are, so you might as well."

"Ye sure?" Little Stevie eyed her curiously.

She nodded. "I'm sure. Fill that belly of yours as best you can."

He did not need to be told twice.

Tucking his legs underneath him, he scooped gelatinous globules of gruel onto the bread and devoured the lot as though it were a box of luxurious sweetmeats. Ada observed him for a minute or two, unable to stop a smile from forming. He reminded her so much of Joshua and Jacob, and the sight of him proved bittersweet.

"How come ye and the other ladies 'round this part of the workhouse have to wear that yellow dress when me ma and the other ladies don't?" Little Stevie asked through a mouthful of crumbs and gruel.

Ada looked down at the dirtied yellow fabric. "Do you remember me telling you about Mrs. Chattoway, the day you brought me here?"

Little Stevie nodded, his dark blue eyes alert. If he had born to a wealthier family, with greater opportunity, she imagined he would have been able to make something of himself. He was smarter than most boys his age and had a maturity about him that made her wonder if he had lived a few lives on this Earth before this one. An old soul, as her mother would have called him.

"That's why," Ada explained, keeping it as vague as she could. "It's so the others can mark us out as... ruined women, and it's probably why you shouldn't be near me."

Little Stevie shrugged. "I don't care what ye did afore ye came here. Everyone's just tryin' to scrape by, ain't they? At least ye didn't do anythin' proper bad, else ye'd be in the jail. As long as ye didn't hurt no-one, why should ye have to look different?"

Ada chuckled. "You're a surprising boy, do you know that? Your ma is lucky to have you."

And I'm lucky you found me when you did.

"She don't think so," he replied, polishing off the last of his dinner. "I'm just a mouth to feed, ye know? But when I get out of here and I get meself one of them apprenticeships somewhere, I'm goin' to show her I were worth havin'. I'm goin' to get us a house and everythin'."

Ada admired his youthful enthusiasm and felt somewhat glad that the world had not yet robbed him of his hopefulness. There were so many children in this workhouse who had lost the light in their eyes, and simply spent their days staring at the wall, or going through the motions of the work they were expected to do.

"Oh, that's what I came to tell ye!" Little Stevie perked up and tapped the side of his head. "I asked around for them boys ye wanted to find. No-one's heard of a Joshua and Jacob Blair, but one man said they might've heard of 'em from a few years back, when he used to give messages and errands for boys to run."

Ada's heart sank. "That'll be from before I got taken away. That's what they used to do." She scooped up a spoonful of gruel and swallowed it straight down. "You could do that, if you speak to the right people. The money won't get you and your ma that house, but it'll be a start."

"Ye think?" He looked excited at the prospect.

"There are folks who'll always need something running across London, so I don't see why not."

She swallowed another spoonful. "Thank you for asking around for me, Stevie. I'd have done it myself, but folks don't like to see a girl in yellow approaching them."

Stevie smiled. "I'll keep askin' when new people come in." He paused. "I hope ye find 'em, whoever they are."

"They're my brothers," Ada admitted quietly. "My ma abandoned us, and I took a risk I shouldn't have. It took me away from those boys. They were everything to me, and they don't know what happened to me, and I don't even know if they're alive."

The boy's expression saddened. "I'm sorry, Ada. I didn't know." He dipped his chin to his chest, as though he were praying. "I'll definitely keep askin', and maybe, one of these days, ye'll find 'em again and it'll be like no time ever passed. If ye tell 'em what happened to ye, they'll forgive ye. That's what family does."

"You must be the most hopeful boy I've ever met." Ada gave a tight chuckle, part of her wishing she had the same optimism as him.

He flashed her a grin. "That's what me ma says an' all, though she don't sound as happy about it."

"What did ye just say about me, Steven Jasper?" a sharp, angry voice seemed to strike a bolt through the boy. He jumped up abruptly, bowl in hand, and turned around to face an equally furious-looking woman in a thin brown dress. His mother, by the looks of it.

Little Stevie bowed his head. "I didn't say nothin', Ma. I were talkin' about someone else."

The boy's mother swiped at his head, catching him on the side of the head. "That's for lyin' to me face." She swiped him again. "And that's for creepin' around where I told ye not to go. This ain't no place for a child." The woman threw a sour glance at Ada and made a thick, hocking sound in the back of her throat. The next thing Ada knew, a glob of spit was hurtling her way. It hit her in the chest, warm and wet and foul, and she shuddered as she felt it slide down her skin.

"Ma!" Little Stevie shouted in horror. "She ha'nt done aught wrong!"

His mother sneered. "If that were true, she wouldn't be wearin' yellow." She grabbed her son by the arm and shoved him away from the partitioned section. He cast an apologetic look back at Ada before he shuffled off, rubbing his smarting head. But it seemed the boy's mother was not finished with Ada.

"Don't blame him. He was only trying to do good," Ada said hurriedly, in the hopes of lessening Little Stevie's later punishment.

"He shouldn't be anywhere near the likes of ye, ye disgustin' wench," the mother hissed. "He don't realise that whores like ye aren't deservin' of charity. The rest of us manage right enough without havin' to sell ourselves, and I don't want ye poisonin' his mind that what ye women do is forgivable. It ain't. Do ye know how many women in this place already hate ye? Ye ruin marriages, ye lead men astray, and we don't want ye and yer sort here, when there are honest folks bein' turned away, who are actually worthy of a roof over they heads and food in they bellies."

Ada hung her head. "I'm sorry."

"Aye, and ye damn well should be." Little Stevie's mother stepped forward and kicked the bowl of gruel that had been resting on Ada's blanket. It sailed through the air, its contents spilling all over Ada's makeshift bed, robbing her of a meal and a vaguely clean place to sleep in one fell swoop. "If I see me boy here again, or ye try to speak to 'im, I'll make sure ye get yerself kicked out of here sharpish. Do ye understand?"

Ada nodded. "I do."

With a scowl that could have pickled blood, the boy's mother stormed off, leaving Ada to try and clean up the mess that had been made. She started with the spit, wiping it away with her sleeve, before turning over her blankets to try and mask the spilled gruel. She would never be able to get it out of the fabric, anyway, and her personal laundry was limited to once a month, though she spent her days, from sunrise to sunset, washing clothes and sheets and cloths for others. She contemplated trying to slip her blanket in with the day's endless laundry, but she knew it would not be worth the penalty if she was discovered.

"Pay her nay mind," another yellow-clad woman nearby whispered across to Ada. "Only difference between us and her is, she ain't been desperate enough, nor low enough, to do what we done."

Ada mustered one of her rehearsed smiles. "I'll not take it to heart."

"Aye, good for ye. That's the way to get through this." The woman turned her back on Ada and, within seconds, the sound of snoring could be heard from her blankets.

But I'm not like you, and I'm not like Stevie's ma. I'm not like either kind that's in here. It was something she had realised, though she had only been here for a few days. The other ladies in yellow had become prostitutes out of necessity, because they had no other way to feed themselves and their families. For Ada, she had been forced into it by a wealthy vulture who had seized an opportunity to extort her and use her for everything she had.

Once upon a time, I was the one spurning my ma for being like this. That seemed like a lifetime ago, and though she might not have felt as though she fit amongst these yellow-dressed women, there was one constant that set them apart from her mother. They still talked about their families. Some of them had their children here with them. Those who were mothers were still mothers, and would have gone back out on the streets to sell themselves again and again, if it meant they could put food on the table for their starving children. But Ada's mother had just... given up.

Feeling despondent, her stomach gnawing with hunger, Ada decided to follow the example of the woman closest and turned over to try and get some sleep. After all, the sooner she drifted off, the sooner she could wake and take the edge off her hunger with a bowl of thin porridge. This time, she hoped she would be able to eat it. If not, the ceaseless day of hard labour to come could well kill her.

Chapter Seventeen

Ada mopped her brow with the back of her forearm, taking a moment to catch her breath before she resumed her work. Out of the corner of her eye, she caught the overseer watching her. Not wanting to get reprimanded, she gripped the large metal pole that served as a stirrer and dragged it around and around the vast cauldron that provided their daily gruel.

"No stoppin'!" the overseer yelled, his eyes fixed on Ada. The men who ran this workhouse always kept a particularly intent eye on the women wearing yellow. No doubt, they thought they might be able to gain favours in return for leniency, but Ada would rather have continued stirring this pot without pause than give them any part of herself.

"What's got his trousers all twisted?" muttered Sally Vaughan, the prostitute who had offered Ada some solace after the assault from Little Stevie's mother.

"Not much, by the look of 'im!" Another 'scarlet lady' cackled as she took out a fresh batch of bread that would not be eaten until they had turned stale.

A ripple of amusement circled around the kitchen, where most of the yellow-dressed women worked when they were not cleaning the workhouse from top to bottom. Ada did not join in with the laughter, lest she draw too much unwanted attention to herself.

Keep your head down. Don't cause any fuss. Don't make any mistakes. She repeated the words over and over in her mind, for she had learned, during the month that she had been here, that it was best to stay quiet and do her work. Not that she had any strength for anything else, when the day was done, and her muscles were screaming from the agony of so much exertion. Even the morning porridge and the evening gruel, paired with a stale cut of bread, barely replenished her reserves.

"Ye got a nasty shiner on yer face there, Ada. Which one of 'em did it to ye? We'll make sure to drop somethin' nasty in his dinner." Sally gave Ada a nod of concern, shining a light on the bruise that dappled her skin from the top of her cheekbone and up her temple. Her punishment yesterday afternoon for not polishing the woodstoves the way the overseer liked.

Ada covered the injury with her hand. She had tried to keep it hidden since it happened with the front part of her hair, but Sally had eyes like a hawk. "It's nothing. I can't remember which one of them hit me, but it's fine. It'll heal soon enough."

"Aye, until ye get another one!" Sally crowed. "Even in the brothel, I weren't treated like this."

An older woman, by the name of Doris Noakes, snorted. "Then why don't ye go back there and give the rest of us' ears a rest from yer whingein'? If I didn't hear ye complainin', I wouldn't know what time of day it is."

"Then I'm doin' ye a service," Sally shot back, with a grin. Despite everything, there was an undeniable camaraderie between prostitutes, especially when they were not competing for money.

"Maybe so, but ye leave Ada out of her cawin'." Doris flashed Ada a smile. "She's the one what'll get smacked if the overseers hear ye talkin' like that. They're too afraid of ye to be hittin' ye, Sally, but they ain't scared of our Ada."

Sally wafted a cloth at the bread to cool the loaves. "I'm tryin' to make her scary, Doris, so they won't pick on her no more. I'm doin' a service to her an' all."

"You don't need to," Ada replied. "I'm really all right. It's only if they touch me that I'll be hollering for you."

Sally chuckled. "An' I'll come runnin', I promise ye!"

"We all will," Doris confirmed, mustering a bubble of assent from the congregation of yellow dresses.

As soon as she heard those words, tears began to well in Ada's eyes. By some strange twist of fate, they were the happiest tears she had shed since she had been freed from Mr. Beauregard's prison. For so long, she had been looking for her family, to no avail, and now it seemed she had found a new one, in the strangest of places. If only she could hear word of her brothers, she knew she would allow herself to feel content in this new life, surrounded by women who would support her through any hardship to come.

~ ~ ~ ~ ~

The following morning, Ada found herself being shaken awake by Sally. She blinked in surprise, disoriented by the unusual interruption. Ordinarily, no-one awoke before the siren that sounded throughout the workhouse, to instruct them all to and eat their breakfast and then get to work.

"Ada, get up!" Sally urged.

Ada rubbed her sleepy eyes. "What is it? What's happened?"

"New 'yellow' got brought in last night. I didn't think nothin' of it 'til she started groanin' and cryin' in the wee hours. I goes over to get her to shut up, thinkin' she's just havin' the usual workhouse weepies, but then I sees her. She's sick as a dog, Ada, and the overseers won't do aught for her," Sally explained as rapidly as her lips and tongue could flap. "I asked 'em and they said, "She's a whore. Don't matter to us if she lives or dies. Be less mouths to feed if she goes on her way." I need ye to come look at her."

Ada frowned. "Why me?"

"Ye said ye helped yer ma and yer brothers when they got sick with marsh fever. I ain't sayin' that's what's up with this woman, but I figure ye'll have a better idea of what to do than the rest of us." Sally grabbed Ada by the wrist and hauled her to her feet. "We been tryin' wet cloths and smellin' salts since I saw her needin' help, but it ain't doin' no good."

Stumbling slightly, as she tried to shake off the sleepiness that weighed down her limbs, Ada followed Sally across the prostitute's quarters. Skirting around a second rudimentary partition on the farthest side, Ada came to an abrupt, heart-stopping halt.

There, lying upon filthy blankets with feverish red cheeks, shaking violently and sweating so hard her dress was drenched through, was her mother.

"Ada?" Sally gave her a curious look. "What's the matter? Ye know this woman? She work at yer brothel?"

Ada reached out to hold onto the mouldy partition, her stomach churning with nausea. Since the moment her mother had abandoned them, she had vowed to remain true to her hatred of the woman, unwilling to give her a smidgen of leniency for her actions.

But it had been easier to hate from afar, believing she would never see her mother again. Now, her mother was here, gravely ill, and Ada did not know what to do. She could not think or move or focus. She could only stand there, shaking as though she were the one with the fever.

"Ada?" Sally repeated, more forcefully.

Ada heaved in an unsteady breath. "It's... my ma."

"What?" Sally's eyes widened.

"The ma who left me and my brothers. That's her." Ada tried blinking fast, to see if it might alter the scene in front of her. Perhaps she was seeing things because of her own fatigue, or because she had been woken so suddenly. Maybe, she was still dreaming.

Sally gave a low whistle. "Then... ye go back to yer bed. I'll keep doin' the cloths and whatnot and let ye know if she gets better."

"No. No, it's all right. I... should help, shouldn't I?" Ada's head swarmed with a thousand conflicting thoughts.

The image of her mother packing up clothes and belongings, with nothing close to an apology. The memory of being so desperate for a meal that she had gone with Mr. Beauregard. The last kisses on the forehead that she had given to her brothers before she had gone out on that fateful day. But then there were the memories of her mother holding them all close in front of the fireplace, at their Isle of Dogs lodgings, and telling them fantastical stories of legendary heroes and mythical creatures. Memories of her mother diving into the water to try and save Etta. Memories of her mother standing up to those brutes on the marshland and gaining a blow to the face for her troubles. The good and the bad, colliding head-on.

Sally shrugged. "I don't agree with what she done, but she's still yer ma. It's up to ye what ye want to do."

"I need hot water and salt," Ada said, after a moment's hesitation. "Can you get that from the kitchens for me?"

Sally nodded. "I'll be quick as I can. Ye need aught else?"

"Vinegar if you can find it." Ada urged her mind to calm. If it did not, she would not be able to concentrate on the task at hand.

"Be back soon." Sally slipped away into the shadows, leaving Ada alone with her mother. Something Ada had never thought would happen again, for as long as she lived.

Slowly, Ada approached the figure on the floor, and knelt beside the foetid blankets. It took her a few moments more to actually reach for her mother's curled-up, trembling hand. With her other hand, Ada pressed her palm to her mother's forehead, and recoiled in alarm. This was no ordinary marsh fever.

The skin was much too hot, and there was a bluish tint to her mother's lips, borne of the croaking, rasping breaths that rattled from the older woman's chest.

"Ma?" Ada said tentatively, tightening her grip on her mother's hand. "Ma, can you hear me?"

The older woman's eyelids fluttered. "Who's there?"

"It's me, Ma." Ada swallowed thickly. "It's Ada. Do you know where you are?"

"At the Ruby Garter... I'm in... my room there," her mother replied, through harsh breaths.

Ada squeezed her eyes shut, realising things were much worse than she had thought. When delirium set in, a fever could go one of two ways: it could break, or it could take a life. "No, Ma, you're not. You're at the workhouse. You must've come here by yourself. Don't you remember?"

"The... workhouse? Why... would I be in the... workhouse?" she panted. "I'm at home. I'm... by the... fire. My boys... are asleep, and my... eldest is brewing up... some tea for us. We're going... to drink it together, like... we do every night when the boys... go to sleep." Her face twisted in a mask of confusion. "But... Etta's not here. Where's... Etta? She was in... my arms, and now... she's not. Did something happen to... her?"

Tears prickled Ada's eyes, as she held tighter to her mother's hand. "Etta's gone, Ma. She drowned years ago."

"Drowned?" Her mother's bottom lip wobbled. "Yes... she did, didn't she? My Ada and... I buried her on... the riverbank. We searched... for days, 'til we... found her."

She paused, rasping violently. "Do you know where my Ada is? Are my... boys asleep? Where are they?"

"You left us, Ma." Ada struggled to hold onto the emotions she had been suppressing for over two years. The pain, the resentment, the hope, all of it. "You went to the brothel, and you left us all alone. Joshua, Jacob, me... you just walked out."

Her mother's eyelids cracked open. "I... left my children?"

"Yes, Ma. You said we'd be better off without you, and you went off to live your life at the brothel. You didn't care what happened to us."

Ada bit the inside of her cheek to try and ease the bitter edge in her voice. "I don't know what's happened to the boys, but I'm here, and I'm wearing a yellow dress because you put me in harm's way. I got snatched off the street because you made us desperate."

Her mother turned slightly, fixing Ada with a bleary gaze. "Ada... is that you?"

"Yes, it's me. I told you it was me."

"What are you doing... here? You're supposed to be... with the boys. You're supposed to be... taking care of... them." Her mother's breath hitched. "I put them... in your care. Where are they? Where are my boys?"

Ada's expression hardened. "You didn't *put* them in my care. You gave us no choice but to struggle through together, and I made a mistake because I wanted them to have one night where their stomachs weren't growling so loud that I couldn't sleep!"

She gasped in shallow, angry breaths. "You have no idea what I've been through because you left us. I've suffered more than you can imagine. You *chose* to sell yourself. I didn't. I was taken, I was knocked unconscious, and I was... ruined night after night, and there was nothing I could do about it!"

"My girl... Don't be cross with me." Her mother managed to squeeze Ada's hand. "You're right. I did... wrong. I remember now."

Ada raised a dubious eyebrow. "You do?"

"I shouldn't have... left you. If you asked me... a thousand times, I wouldn't... be able to tell you why... I did it." Her mother grimaced, as though she were in pain. "I thought... you would... all be better without me. I couldn't... carry on. I needed my gin. I needed to... not feel. You all made... me feel too much. I knew I... was failing you, and I couldn't... face it. After we lost our spot, it was... the last blow... I could take. I was a... coward, and I stopped being... a mother to you all. I put you... in that position instead, and I stopped... thinking and caring. I didn't want to feel anymore."

Ada observed her mother's feverish face. "That's why you left?"

"It's... the only way... I can explain it." She paused. "But... the boys. Where are the boys? Did you lose them?"

Ada hung her head. "I got taken away by a cruel man, and I was locked up for two years. They wouldn't let me see my brothers, and they wouldn't give me news of them. I tried to find out what happened to them when I finally got my freedom, but no-one knows anything. It's like they vanished, or worse."

"You're... not to blame, my girl." Her mother's eyes focused briefly. "You love those boys, more... than any mother could. I'm sorry... I put you all at risk. It's my fault this... happened to you all. It's my fault... you were taken. It's my fault... the boys have gone. I wasn't a ma to you. No ma leaves their children alone."

A heavy sob wracked Ada's chest. "You shouldn't try to speak too much, Ma. You're not well. You should rest, and get better, and we can talk about the boys and everything else when you're well again."

"I won't be getting better, my girl," her mother confessed. "They... kicked me out of the Ruby. They said I... have consumption. I were coughing up blood for months. I tried... to keep it quiet, so no-one would know. One of the girls... told the Madam, and I got... sent away. That's why... I came here."

Ada froze. "No... No, you can't have consumption. That's not right. You're delirious, that's all. You don't know what you're saying."

In that moment, all of the hatred she had been clinging onto, drained out of her body in a helpless rush.

It was simpler to despise a person when they were not lying sick on wretched blankets, in a dripping workhouse, with lungs that were close to giving out.

As Ada looked down at her mother, all she could think about were the brighter memories, and all her mother had endured. It would be enough to make anyone want to escape, for fear that they might lose everyone else they had left.

"I know I don't have much longer," her mother murmured. "And I know... you must hate me, but... I'm glad you're here. I'm glad... I somehow found you, after... everything. I'm glad... I don't have to be alone, at the end, even though... that's probably what I... deserve."

Ada lifted her mother's hands to her lips and kissed them gently. "Don't say that, Ma. No matter what you did, you'd never deserve to die alone." She sucked in a breath. "And you're not going to die. You're going to be fine. I'm going to help you, the way I helped you all when you got sick on from the water."

"This isn't the same. We both know—" A violent cough erupted from her mother's mouth, severing her sentence. Panicking, Ada lunged forward and bundled her mother into her arms, so she might breathe easier. Instead, her mother wheezed and spluttered, her thin frame shuddering in Ada's grasp, to the point where Ada could feel every movement through her mother's bony ribcage.

"Just breathe, Ma. You have to breathe!" Ada cried, rubbing her mother's back and willing the coughing to ease. But it would not, and soon, Ada spied the vivid red of blood splattering down her mother's chin and trickling from the corners of her mouth.

At that moment, Sally returned with empty arms and a nasty lump on her cheek that seemed to be darkening and spreading down beneath her eye by the second. She offered Ada a sorrowful expression.

"I got caught, and I got hit," Sally explained. "I tried tellin' 'em what was goin' on, but they didn't want to hear it. They said it would be a waste of heat and salt."

Ada held onto her mother. "You did your best."

"Is she... goin' to be all right?" Sally eyed Ada's mother dubiously.

"No, I don't think so. She's consumptive."

Ada struggled to force out the words, unwilling to accept the stark reality behind them. It seemed too cruel to have found her mother again, and heard her explanation for the abandonment, only to have her taken away again.

Sally nodded slowly. "Ah, I'm sorry, Ada. That's rough." She pointed over her shoulder. "Do ye want me to go?"

"If you don't mind?"

Ada did not want anyone to see her in the throes of grief, nor did she want anyone watching her mother suffer through the pains of these volatile coughs. Her mother had likely suffered enough indignity whilst working at the brothel. She did not need any more at the end of her days.

Sally leaned down and gave Ada's shoulder a friendly squeeze. "Ye call me if ye need anythin' else. I'm just sorry I couldn't get any of what ye asked for."

"I don't think I could've fixed this, even if you had been able to," Ada assured, attempting to maintain a strong façade, if only until she was alone with her mother again.

With that, Sally left, just as Ada's mother launched into another brutal bout of coughing. Ada had not been around many people with consumption, but she had seen enough people die. And this sounded an awful lot like a death rattle.

Indeed, she realised with a heavy heart that there was nothing she could except put her arms around her mother and offer comfort until the end finally came. Even if it took all night, Ada was determined not to move for anything.

"Can you… ever forgive me?" her mother wheezed, during a fleeting reprieve.

Ada clutched her mother close.

"I do forgive you. I can't speak for the boys, but I forgive you. I didn't understand back then, but… I think I do, now. You were in pain. You were hurting. You wanted to avoid the things that made you feel. You weren't a coward, Ma, you were just… troubled, and you didn't want to put that on us."

"I don't deserve you, Ada," her mother whispered. "I love you. I love you, my girl."

Ada buried her face in her mother's sweat-dampened hair.

"I love you, too. How can you not deserve me, when you gave me life? There are things we all wish we'd done differently, but we can't change that, now. I couldn't hold a grudge, even if I wanted to."

"Try and think of me… fondly, sometimes. And please, don't… ever blame yourself. It's not your f—"

Another vicious cough bombarded her mother's lungs, her body spasming wildly in Ada's arms as she tried to physically hold her mother together.

As if, if she just clasped tight enough, and willed strongly enough, they would be granted a miracle.

Unfortunately, the world did not offer miracles to people like Ada and her mother, who saw a glint in river mud and called it gold. And as dawn rose, cold and misty, through the smeared workhouse windows, Ada was left weeping over the husk of her mother, whose soul had already moved on to a better place.

"I love you, Ma," she whispered, wiping the salty tears from her face as she placed a tender, parting kiss upon her mother's icy cheek.

Silence echoed from stilled lips. And just like that, she was alone again.

Chapter Eighteen

Life in the workhouse did not stop for death or illness or tragedy, and a fortnight later, that final night with her mother seemed like a distant dream to Ada. With no money, she had not been able to afford a proper grave for the woman who had given her life.

Instead, her mother had an etched stone, barely more than a pebble, in the vast yard around the back of the workhouse where all the paupers were loaded into the earth en-masse, as worthless in death as they had been deemed in life. It was the only marker Ada had, to remind her where her mother had been laid to rest, though she did not often get a moment to visit the spot.

As always, Ada awoke early, ate her morning porridge, and took to the day's work with all the energy she could muster. The back-breaking labour served to take her mind off that pitiful grave in the yard, and the lost boys who still haunted her, though she could not chase the thoughts away when night came.

One morning, she had been tasked with cleaning the front steps of the winter filth. She did not see the point, when it would only become covered in dirt again, but at least it gave her something to do.

Having scrubbed for the better part of two hours, without realising the passage of time, she paused to wipe the sweat from her brow. A chilly breeze swept up from the London streets, pinching at her warmed cheeks, and prompting her to turn into it to refresh herself. She closed her eyes and let it wash over her, as invigorating as splashing her face with cold water.

"Ada?" A low, masculine voice called out her name, startling her out of her peaceful reverie. She felt certain an overseer had caught her idling and was seconds from striking her for laziness.

However, when she opened her eyes, her mouth fell open in shock. "Elijah?"

He looked older, all of the boyish fleshiness gone from his face, revealing more angular cheekbones and a strong jaw. His shoulders were broader than she remembered, and he seemed taller, with the appearance of a man instead of a boy. In his hands, he held a hammer and chisel, and appeared to have been working on some masonry by the front gates.

He must still be working for his pa. It pleased her and saddened her in equal measure, for she realised that if she had just swallowed her fear and her pride, and had gone to his stonemasonry workshop the day she was dragged into the alley, she might have avoided so much unpleasantness. Or, perhaps, she would have faced his disdain, so she could avoid it now.

Still holding onto his tools, he approached her uncertainly. "Is it really you?" She noticed his eyes flickering down towards her dress, and the surprise in his expression as he observed the yellow colour. He would know what it meant, she felt sure of it.

"It's me," she confirmed, though she had contemplated lying for just a moment.

He nodded up at the workhouse. "What are you doing here?"

"It's a long story." She folded her arms across her chest, as though she could somehow conceal the yellow of her dress entirely.

He canted his head. "I have the time to listen."

"I don't even know where to begin," she confessed, her heart pounding, her cheeks burning with shame. "Do you remember I used to collect cigar ends?"

He nodded: his expression unreadable. "Of course."

"Well, I encountered a man that I shouldn't have trusted, whilst I was collecting those ends." Slowly but surely, the whole tale began to unfurl, beginning with Mr. Beauregard, his cruel trick, and her mistake in allowing him to manipulate her neediness. She moved onto how she had fought to be free, and had even asked them to kill her, if they would not let her go or tell her where her brothers were.

From there, she continued the story with her eventual liberation, the theft and assault in the alley, and the shame that had prevented her from going to Elijah's workshop. Finally, she concluded with her life upon the streets, Little Stevie's angelic actions, and the recent loss of her mother.

By the end of it all, she was breathless with emotion, tears rolling down her cheeks and dropping onto the stone porch that she had just scrubbed. "I think that's about it, but I still don't know where my brothers are."

For a long while, he was silent, giving nothing away upon his handsome features. All Ada could do was stand there and watch him, bracing herself for the torrent of disgust and loathing that she fully expected to hear from him. How could he not think ill of her, when she was standing before him in a yellow dress, at the front of a workhouse, with such a sordid, terrible tale trailing behind her like a cloud of filth? She was not the Ada he had known. That Ada was long dead, with no headstone to mark her passing.

So, it came as quite the surprise when a small, sad smile turned up the corners of his lips. "I wondered what happened to you. I asked around for you, for a while, but no-one could tell me anything. It was like you disappeared one day and never came back."

"I did, in many ways," she said quietly. "What about you? I see you're still working with stone."

He nodded. "I made my mastery, but I still work alongside my pa at the shop. Not much has changed for me, except I don't get daily visits from my dearest friend anymore." He sighed as though he had the weight of the world on his shoulders. "I knew you wouldn't have left London without saying goodbye to me. I just... I just wish you'd come to me that day, when you got attacked. I wouldn't have turned you away, I swear. If my pa had even tried, I would've followed you out of there and never gone back."

"I couldn't. That day, I wasn't even sure I wanted to live anymore." She swallowed the growing lump in her throat, wondering what could have been if she had acted differently. Might there have been hope for them, if she had just forced herself to go to him that day? She supposed she would never know.

He stepped closer and tried to take her hand, prompting her to recoil. "I'm so sorry, Ada. I'm so sorry for what you've been through." He took his hand back. "I understand why you probably don't want any man to touch you, so I won't. I just want you to know that I was thinking about you. I've never forgotten you, and if I'd known the trouble you were in, I would've battered down that fellow's door and wrung his neck to get you out of there."

"What's done is done," she mumbled tearfully.

"Maybe so, but there is something I *can* change." He held her gaze, his eyes swimming with sadness. "I don't smoke cigars, but I am willing to help you, however I can, if you want to leave this workhouse right now. Let me make it right, Ada. Please."

You have no idea how I've longed to hear you say that... How I've longed for you to come along and say you'll save me. But I can't do that to you. I'm not worth saving anymore.

She lowered her gaze, unable to witness his expression. "You can't make it right, Elijah. No-one can. It's too many years too late for anyone to help me." She knew she could not run into his arms and be the cheerful, innocent Ada she had been when they used to meet one another in his father's workshop.

She wanted to, of course she did, but she could not bring herself to do it.

"Ada, please. Let me take you out of here. I can find somewhere for you to rest, and heal, and recover. I'm not asking for anything from you, I just want to be able to help in a way I haven't been able to since you disappeared," he urged, taking another step towards her.

She backed off. "I'm sorry, Elijah... I just can't. There's nothing left of me to heal."

"Ada..." He put out his hands, as if he were going to take hers in his, but he did not touch her. "That is nonsense. You're alive! To me, it's like you've come back from the dead. So, please, let me take care of you."

"Pretend you never saw me," she said, more firmly. "I think that'd best for you and for me."

Unable to bear his pleas any longer, in case she crumbled, she picked up her bucket of soapy water and her scrubbing brush and hurried inside before he could stop her.

Forgive me, Elijah. Please, forgive me.

$\sim \sim \sim \sim \sim$

Later that evening, Sally came to sit beside Ada in her corner of the prostitute's quarters. She came bearing some extra, stale bread that she had managed to pilfer from the kitchens without being seen.

"Who was that lad I saw ye talkin' to earlier?" Sally asked, without preamble.

Ada took the proffered chunk of bread and began to soften a piece in her mouth. "An old friend. He wants to help me."

"Handsome lookin' friend ye got there. When ye say friend, do ye mean 'lover'?"

Ada shook her head. "I used to think we'd be married, but then I got taken, and everything changed. He deserves better than me."

"Who says?" Sally chewed on her bread.

"He's a good man. He always was. He should be with someone... whole, instead of someone who's like this bread—all stale and broken." Ada sank back against the grimy wall. "It's better that I let him go."

Sally frowned. "I know ye been hurt, girl, but a lad like that don't come along too often. If he likes ye, and he wants to take ye out of this pit, then ye should go runnin' into his arms and never look back. That's what I'd do."

"You're braver than me," Ada replied.

"Pfft, that ain't true. I watched ye sit at yer ma's bedside all night, holdin' her hand, when she's the one what got ye into this mess, in a twisted sort of way. Ye stayed with her, in her last hours, after everythin' she done. If that ain't bravery, then I don't know what is." Sally gave her a nudge in the arm, but she would not be swayed.

"I won't change my mind," Ada protested. "Even if I went with him, what good would it do? I'd never trust him. It doesn't matter that he's a good man. He's still a man, and I can't be near any of them. It makes me flinch."

Sally softened her expression. "Then ye give it time. It heals most everythin', if ye let it. And he seems willin' to try." She nodded towards the front doors in the distance. "He's still out there now. All the ladies been watchin' 'im from the hall, 'til the overseers came and ruined everyone's fun."

"He's still there?" Ada's eyes widened in shock.

"Seems he ain't ready to give up on ye, even if ye've given up on yerself." Sally shuffled over to her own blankets, and flashed Ada one last, pointed look. "Think about it, that's all I'm sayin'. Every woman in here, wearin' a yellow dress, would give everythin' to be able to leave on the arm of a good man. So, ye think about it long and hard. Maybe, he'll still be there in the mornin' and I can see ye off with a smile on me face."

As she turned over and soundly fell asleep, Ada stared at the distant doors and wondered... Did she still have a hope of happiness, after all?

Chapter Nineteen

Day after day, Elijah had a way of finding Ada. It did not matter if she asked for tasks in the kitchen, or weeding the graveyard, or scrubbing the farthest wall until it shone, he would somehow appear to perform some repair or masonry endeavour within her vicinity.

Sometimes, he did not say a word to her, and simply watched her out of the corner of his eye. Sometimes, he tried to converse, with varying degrees of success. Sometimes, he gave her offerings of food, disguised as something he had not been able to finish eating.

"You should make sure your hands stay dry at the end of the day," he said one afternoon, a fortnight after she had first encountered him on the porch. "Otherwise they'll crack and get sores, like on your thumb."

She stared down at her hand and saw the blistered flesh. "It's hard to, when everything's damp all the time."

"Take this to help." From the leather bag where he kept his tools, he produced a candlestick and holder, with a box of matches to go with it. "Oh, and you should have this, too. I couldn't finish it." He added a small parcel of something to the candle gifts and held them out to her.

She frowned. "You don't have to keep doing this."

"Doing what? It'll only go to waste if you don't have it," he replied, with that sweet, boyish look upon his face that she remembered so well. In truth, it made it impossible to refuse his disguised gifts.

"I'm not stupid, Elijah," she said, not unkindly. "I know you're trying to help me, but you're just doing it sneakily."

He feigned ignorance. "I don't know what you're talking about. I packed too much for my luncheon, and I would rather you had it than the rats."

Reluctantly, she took the gifts. "Thank you, Elijah. But, surely, you must be finished fixing things here? I know the workhouse is falling to pieces, but you can't repair everything."

"Can't I?" He smiled broadly, and her heart swelled just a smidgen. As though it had stopped beating and had just been coaxed back into life.

She turned her face away. "You really should forget about me, Elijah. No good can come of this. I have people here who are taking care of me, and they don't spurn me.

They know what I am, and they know what I've been through, and they make sure I'm all right."

"I don't spurn you, Ada," he said, as though wounded. "I would never. You're not at fault for what happened to you. I blame the man who tricked you, and I'm still determined to find him and wring his neck. But you wanted to help your brothers; how could I ever look down on that?"

Ada furrowed her brow. "The things that have been done to me... How could you not spurn that?"

"If you were ridden down by horses, and you were injured, would I show you disdain? No. Would I blame you or the horses? I'd blame the horses. It's the same thing," he insisted in earnest. "You were wounded, and now I want to take care of you. I have the money and I have the ability. But, more than that, I have the desire. I *want* to help you."

Ada shook her head. "You'd only ever see me as this pitiful, ruined, broken creature. I don't want to be that to you."

"How do you know that?" He gazed at her with a sweetness in his eyes. "Are you in my head? I don't think you're pitiful. I think you're incredibly strong and brave, and though I can't pretend to understand the breadth of what you've suffered, I *can* be there to help you through the rest of your days. I don't want anything more than that."

At that moment, Sally unleashed an almighty sigh. "Ada Blair, if ye don't take that man's hand and get yerself out of this workhouse, I'm goin' to run off with him meself, and that's somethin' neither ye nor him wants!"

Mortified, Ada raised her hands, palm up. "Ignore her. She's half mad."

"And ye're all mad if ye don't go with 'im!" Sally retorted, smirking.

Elijah smiled shyly. "Then, perhaps you'll consider this. I recently bought the house next to the workshop, and I thought you and I might live there. You would have your own bedchamber, and though we will need to be married, it will only be for propriety's sake. I am not asking anything more than that of you.

I just want to be close to you, so I can help when you need. And whilst we're living there together, I want to offer my services to help find your brothers, too. *When* we find them, I'll make them into mason's apprentices, and they will have a home in the workshop as they learn a trade that will see them successful for the rest of their lives. That is what I'm offering you, and asking nothing in return, other than your assent to be my wife."

Ada stared at him in disbelief. "You don't want to marry me, Elijah! How could you want a woman like me? Find someone pure and untouched and loving, who can be the wife you deserve."

"You're the wife I want, Ada." He smiled hopefully. "I've wanted you to be my wife since I first met you, and that hasn't changed. You're still the only person I could envision spending the rest of my life with, and what you've endured makes me want to shelter you and love you and take care of you more. It doesn't diminish it. So... please say you'll be with me, so that we can begin our lives afresh, together, and find your brothers, and put everything back the way it's supposed to be. It doesn't matter how long it takes. I'm not going anywhere."

Sally burst into raucous applause. "What are ye waitin' for?! Go and live yer life, girl! We don't want ye here no more. Ain't that right, Doris?" She turned to the older woman, who had been eavesdropping with a small circle of the yellow dresses.

"Aye, get yerself out of here before we chase ye out!" Doris crowed, cackling. "And get us all one of these Elijahs when ye're out there, livin' yer life over!"

The other yellow dresses began to applaud, making Ada's cheeks burn with a fiery fury. Deep down, she knew they were right. If this was not her one road out of destitution and despair, then she did not know what was. And, if she accepted, she would be the wife of the only man she had ever considered a suitable husband prospect.

The man she had still dreamed of, even in her darkest moments, as if he had been calling to her for the past two years.

"I don't know, Elijah," she murmured shyly.

He took a step towards her and put out his hand, letting her make the first move. "I love you, Ada. I've loved you all this time, and I've no plans to stop. It broke my heart when you disappeared, and I didn't know what had happened to you. I searched for you more than I told you.

I felt like you were still in London somewhere, but I just couldn't… see you. And then you came back—the love of my life—and we were in the same place, at the same time. If that's not fate, then it doesn't exist."

"What if it's too much? What if I'm too broken?" Her fingers twitched, longing to reach out and take his hand.

He smiled. "I'm a mason. I repair things. If it takes all our lives, I'll do everything I can to put you back together. Though I only see you, as you are, and as you were. You don't look broken to me. You look like my Ada. My love. My only love."

"Get out of here!" Sally and the others roared, evidently about to cause a riot if she did not accept. But, as she gazed into Elijah's eyes, she realised she did not need their coercion. There was nothing but honesty in his gaze, and nothing but earnest truth in his words. He meant it. He loved her. And she would have been a fool to walk away from that.

Gingerly, she reached out and took his hand. "I... accept."

"You do?" His eyes widened.

She nodded. "I do."

And one day, when my heart feels more whole, I'll be able to tell you just how much I love you, too. Just wait, my dear Elijah. Be patient with me.

Accompanied by the deafening cacophony of the rowdy prostitutes, she held tight to Elijah's hand and let him lead her out of the workhouse. And, just as Sally had suggested, she never looked back.

Chapter Twenty

Ada huddled on the bottom step of the wooden staircase; her knees tucked up to her chin. From the kitchen, she heard the sound of Elijah preparing something for them both to eat. He had left the front door open for her, so she could gaze out at the street beyond, and be able to remind herself that she was not a prisoner anymore. She did not have to follow a routine or obey any master other than herself. But the habits she had become so accustomed to were proving difficult to shake off, her body tensed in a state of constant anxiety that she might have her freedom taken away again.

A few minutes later, Elijah appeared in the doorway off to her right, bearing a tray of bread and cheese, and two cups of steaming tea. Simple foods that would not cause Ada any stomach upset.

"You can come into the kitchen, if you want?" he offered, but she shook her head.

"I like it here, where I can see the outside world."

He nodded and came to sit on the floor in front of her. "We could go for a walk, if you feel up to it?"

"Maybe in a few days," she replied. It had only been a week since Elijah had taken her away from the workhouse, and she had not yet dared to set foot over the threshold. She liked to see that she had freedom, but she did not know if she would be able to wander the streets without her worries overwhelming her. At least, not just yet.

He broke off a piece of bread for her, and laid cheese on top, before passing it up to her. She noticed he was always careful not to accidentally touch her hand, for the sake of her comfort.

"Whenever you're ready, Ada," he assured, with a warm smile. "But I thought I might go to Shadwell again, and ask after your brothers. Someone must know where they are, or where they went. I'll keep asking until one of them answers me."

Ada took the food gratefully, and slowly softened it in her mouth. "When I'm rested, I'll come with you. I just don't think my legs will be able to take a long walk today. I'm still getting used to being able to go wherever I want."

"You don't have to do anything until you feel well again." Elijah began to eat his own luncheon. "I'll keep looking for them on your behalf, until your body has healed and you're feeling better about having your life back."

Ada swallowed the food. For the first time in a long while, the bread and cheese was not merely taking the edge of a gnawing and painful hunger; it was adding to the fullness that was already there. Already, some colour had returned to her cheeks, and her stomach looked less concave.

Though she was still being careful with how much she ate at once, in case it made her sick.

"I *am* grateful to you, you know?" Ada said quietly. "It probably doesn't seem like it, but I really am."

He smiled at her. "I know you are, love, but you've nothing to thank me for. I'll always wish I searched for you more insistently, so I could've spared you some of your pain. Think of this as me making amends for some of the hurt you've suffered. I'll keep trying to make amends for the rest of my days."

"It wasn't your fault you couldn't find me, or stop things from happening," she protested, seeing the sorrow in his eyes. "I shouldn't have trusted a wealthy gentleman who dangled a carrot in front of me."

Elijah lowered his gaze. "Even so, you know I meant what I said when I took you away from the workhouse, don't you? We might be married, but I'll never expect or ask anything of you. You're my wife because I love you, that is true, but I also married you because I want to keep you safe. I would never do anything to add to your torments."

Ada had not yet come to terms with the fact that she was a married woman, and she did not think it would seem real for a long time to come. The very next day, after she had left the warehouse, they had wed in the local church, with Elijah's father and an errand boy as witnesses. A small, simple ceremony that had been over with in the blink of an eye. She could not even remember saying the vows, though her heart knew she had spoken them.

Her heart felt loved, and wanted to love Elijah in return, but it was still battle-scarred and broken, and she was not sure when it might begin healing enough to open again.

Gingerly, she reached out and rested a hand on Elijah's shoulder. "I... I... I could only ever imagine being married to you. I hope that, one day, I'll be able to put the past behind me and look forward to a future with you. But I know you're probably the only man I can trust not to hurt me."

They finished the rest of their luncheon in companionable silence, both of them gazing out at the street together. All the while, Ada kept her calf pressed lightly against Elijah's upper arm, just to feel somewhat connected to him. It eased her nerves to have him near, but the fear returned every time he stepped out of the house and closed the door behind him. It did not matter that she knew he would come back and might even do so with her brothers. The sense of being closed in was stronger than her logic.

With their luncheon eaten, Elijah took the tray back through to the kitchen, and reappeared a moment later.

"I won't be too long, I promise," he said, as he made for the door. "I'm going to close this, but only so no-one can get in. You will still be able to get out, if you feel you want to walk or something."

Ada got up off the step and approached him. "Do you swear you'll come back?"

"I swear," he confirmed.

She hesitated, feeling suddenly awkward. "Can you... hold me for a moment, before you go?"

"Are you sure?" He looked at her in surprise.

She nodded. "It might make me feel better."

"Then, of course I can." He held out his arms and let her walk into his embrace. Squeezing her eyes shut, she locked her hands behind his back and buried her face into his neck, inhaling the soapy scent of his shirt collar. It was the first true contact she had actively sought, and she did not know how it would make her feel.

However, as his arms enfolded her in a gentle hold, there was no terror or unease. Instead, his quiet strength made her feel safe, as though she were finally out of danger. Freeing her locked hands so she could clutch him tighter, she realised that she never wanted to let this man go.

He had been one of the only lights in her life when her mother left, and he was here at her side, once again, to hold her together and stop her from falling to pieces after the years of abuse and injury and loss.

"You won't leave me, will you?" she whispered into his shoulder.

He smiled against her hair. "Never, love. Never."

"Then... I suppose I should let you go, shouldn't I?" Reluctantly, she released him.

"I promise I'm coming back," he reassured. "I love you."

She nodded slowly. "Be safe."

"I will." He offered her a parting smile, and stepped out of the house, closing the front door behind him.

Fighting to steady her breaths, Ada shuffled back over to the staircase and sank down on the bottom stop, determined to sit and keep her eyes on the door until Elijah walked through it again.

~ ~ ~ ~ ~

Stiff-legged and half asleep on the stairwell, Ada jolted awake as the front door opened. For a moment, she thought her eyes were still blurred from dozing off, because she was certain she could see three shadows silhouetted in the doorway, instead of just one. Panic came next, her heart racing, for fear that Mr. Beauregard, or Mrs. Chattoway, or even someone at the workhouse, had come to drag her back.

"Ada?" Elijah's voice soothed her rampant nerves, as the sunlight softened his silhouette and revealed his kind face. "I have two people here who are very eager to see you."

Ada rubbed her eyes as the two other silhouettes came into focus. A young boy of perhaps ten stood awkwardly beside an older boy of ten-and-three, maybe older, maybe younger. They were both so slight and malnourished that it was difficult to gauge their ages, and their faces were smeared in so much dirt and muck and filth that it looked as though they had deliberately camouflaged themselves. But there was something familiar about their features, and a slight shine in their wide eyes that struck a flint in her chest, lighting a spark that she had thought to be extinguished long ago.

"L-Little bug? J-Joshie?" she stammered. "Is it really you?" She did not dare to leave her spot on the step, in case it was a mirage, or a cruel dream.

The older boy nodded stiffly. "No-one's called me that in a couple years."

"Ada... You're alive?" The younger boy skirted past Elijah and ran straight for her, launching himself into her arms. Instinctively, she put those arms around him and held him close, not caring a jot for the rancid stench of his tattered clothes, or the dirt that transferred to her pale blue dress. She was holding her little brother. After so long, she was finally holding him in her arms again.

"I'm so sorry," Ada gasped, as the tears came in an almighty flood. "I'm so, so, so, so sorry. You must've been so afraid. You must've thought that I abandoned you. I'm so very sorry. Sorrier than you could know." She hugged him as tight as she could. "I tried to find you, I tried to get word to you, but... I couldn't. No matter what I did, I couldn't get anyone to tell you what happened to me, and by the time I was free, you'd both disappeared and no-one had any answers about where you were, or if you were even still alive."

Joshua began to sob into Ada's shoulder. "We thought ye were dead. Someone said ye'd been run down by a carriage. We didn't think we'd ever see ye again." His little hands clawed at her like a frantic kitten, as though he did not quite believe this was real, either.

It took her a few minutes to realise that Jacob had not stepped forward. He remained behind Elijah, just staring at her. She could not read his expression, his eyes wide and vacant.

Over Joshua's shoulder, she beckoned to him. "Come here, little bug. Come over here and let me hold you."

"Where were ye, all this time?" was all he said, scuffing the holey toe of his boot against the floorboards. "If ye wasn't dead, like we was told, then where were ye?" His voice had become harsher than the last time she had seen him, and he had lost so much of the soft youthfulness in his face. He was still a few years shy of manhood, but there was a cold, distant maturity to him that alarmed Ada. Evidently, she was not the only one who had been through a great deal.

Ada sighed and gently shifted Joshua away from her, so that he could sit beside her on the step. "It's not a nice story, but it's one that you both deserve to hear. I want you to know that I would never have left you, on purpose. I would never have abandoned you, but I acted foolishly, and it has changed everything."

Taking a deep breath, she began to recount the tale. It would have been easy for her to leave out details, in order to spare the boys some of the hardships she had suffered, but she did not want to shelter them from the truth. And so, she told them everything, from beginning to end, leaving nothing out.

She began with Mr. Beauregard, and how she had gone with him to acquire stew for the three of them. She told them how she had been drugged by the stew and held prisoner against her will in a house of ill-repute. She revealed details of the clients who paid for her to be unconscious, and those who beat her, and those who tried to be nice. Details she had not even told Elijah, up to that point. Then she explained how she had been taken to Mr. Beauregard's house to be a prisoner yet again, though she made sure to reiterate how often she had tried to escape, and fight, and beg for word of the boys.

She continued with the theft and attempted rape in the alleyway, and the loss of her money. How that loss had nearly cost her, her life when she had almost frozen to death on the steps of a church. Finally, she finished with her time at the workhouse, and the wretched loss of their mother, and the eventual salvation that Elijah had given her.

"My mistake has cost us all greatly, and I will never be able to apologise enough for that," she concluded, her cheeks damp with tears. "What about the two of you? Where have you been, all this time?"

Jacob mopped tears from his own eyes as he finally came forward and wrapped his arms around his elder sister. "I knew ye'd not leave us on purpose. I blamed ye for months after we heard ye'd died, wishin' ye'd not stepped out into the road and got yerself run down." He hiccoughed. "But I'm glad ye're not dead. I'm not glad for what ye went through, but I'm glad I can see ye again, and be near ye again. I never thought it'd happen 'til me dyin' day."

"I managed to get the landlord to talk," Elijah chimed in, answering for Jacob, who had hidden his face in his sister's shoulder. "He said some man came to the lodgings and told the boys that you'd been killed in an accident. He overheard and kicked the boys out, which is probably why he kept silent for so long. Out of guilt."

Joshua nodded, clinging to Ada's arm. "Jacob said we should go back to the Island. That's where we been ever since. Mudlarkin' and sleepin' in a shelter what Jacob made from half a boat what washed ashore."

"You went back to the Isle of Dogs?" Ada could have cursed herself for not trying there first. Of course they would have returned to the only place they knew of that could offer some sort of income, albeit fickle.

"We wasn't as good at the mudlark business as ye, Sis, but we managed. Didn't we, Joshua?" Jacob raised his head, his tears forming runnels through the mud caked on his face.

I knew I recognised that smell, she realised. She had stunk of the Thames mud so often herself, and yet she had forgotten it.

Joshua scratched his eyebrow. "The winters were cold, but we had us plenty of driftwood for fire. And the tavern ladies would take pity on me a lot and give us some food when we was hungry."

"I can't believe you're both here." Ada looked up at Elijah. "How did you find them after you spoke with the landlord? How did you know where they would be?"

Elijah smiled. "I remembered the stories you used to tell me about that place and wondered if these two might've gone back to somewhere familiar, after they were turfed out of their lodgings. When I asked at the tavern about them, one of the women directed me to their boat hut, and that's where I found them." He paused. "They didn't believe you were alive and well, at first, but I'm pleased I could persuade them, in the end."

"Thank you," she rasped, her throat thick with emotion. "Thank you, thank you, thank you!"

He lowered his gaze shyly. "I was simply keeping my promise to you, love. A wedding gift of sorts."

Jacob stared at Ada, before shifting his eyes to Elijah. "Ye're married to me sister? Ye never said aught about that when ye found us! When did ye get wed?"

"A few days ago," Ada explained. "We wanted to make things proper before I came to live in this house, and so we got married. If I'd known you would be found so soon, I would've waited so you could see our wedding."

Jacob's expression hardened. "Well, ye better treat her right, else there'll be trouble."

"I fully intend to," Elijah assured, with a lopsided smile. "As for the two of you, I would like to offer you both apprenticeships, so that your sister can feel safe in the knowledge that you'll have reliable work for the rest of your days."

Joshua's eyebrows lifted in curiosity. "Apprentices as what?"

"I'm a stonemason, and my workshop is next to this house." Elijah gestured vaguely at the door. "Would that be of interest to you?"

Joshua nodded effusively. "I'd like to do it!"

"Aye, I suppose I wouldn't mind that," Jacob added more coolly, though Ada could tell he was very interested indeed. He had a sparkle in his eyes that had not been there before.

Elijah dipped his head. "Very good, then I'll leave the three of you to reacquaint yourselves, whilst I go and prepare some tea and cake. I think everyone has more than earned it."

As he left the three siblings upon the staircase, Ada scooped both of her brothers back into her arms and held them as tightly as she could, ignoring the burn in her weakened muscles. There was no pain so great that she could not overcome it for the sake of her brothers. And, as she clutched them to her, she knew that she would never let them go again. Just as she would never let Elijah go.

"You came back," she whispered. "All of you... You came back."

Never in her life had sweeter words been spoken. After over two years of fearing the worst, the nightmare was finally over.

Epilogue

Two Years Later...

Ada hummed to herself in the kitchen of her marital home, stirring a rich beef stew for their dinner. The lean days were long behind her, and though she still tried to avoid unnecessary expense, it felt nice to be able to have meat in their evening meal. Elijah ensured that they never went without, and there was always fresh bread, butter, milk, and cheese, alongside ripe vegetables, eggs, and fruit whenever it took Ada's fancy.

She lifted a ladleful to her lips and sipped. The warm, hearty taste filled her mouth, making her smile as she set the lid on top of the pot, so it would be ready for the return of her husband and her brothers.

As though summoned by the delicious scent, she heard the front door open, and the sound of cheerful voices echoing in the hallway.

"I chisel far neater than ye!" Joshua protested, apparently continuing a good-natured competition.

Jacob snorted. "Ye chipped a whole block off!"

"Only 'cause ye were distractin' me," Joshua replied. "Ye were watchin' over me shoulder like a gull wantin' scraps."

Elijah chuckled. "You both have excellent chiselling skills. It is your carving that needs work, but you're getting better by the day."

Ada's heart swelled as she listened to the three of them, content in the knowledge that they were all safe, and loved, and no longer wondering where their next home, or their next meal, or even their next bit of warmth would come from.

It cheered her all the more, knowing how much they adored each other. Elijah had almost become a father to the two boys, and she knew he relished the opportunity to teach them his trade each day and watch them flourish.

I wish you could see us, Ma. I wish you knew that we were all happy, and in good health, and living a life that you could only have dreamt for us.

After the tragic events that had transpired at the workhouse, Ada's forgiveness of her mother had prevailed. It was much easier to continue to forgive someone once safety and joy and love had been achieved, though

Ada's happiness occasionally made her feel guilty, if only because she could not share it with her mother. Ada had managed to save her brothers, but she had not been able to save the woman who gave them all life.

No matter what her mother had done, that would always make her sad sometimes.

"Get yourselves washed and come back down for dinner, before your sister sees the state of your faces," Elijah instructed, with an amused note in his voice. "You're not urchins now."

Joshua chuckled. "We'll never get used to not bein' caked in dirt."

"But I'd rather be covered in stone dust than river muck, any day," Jacob added, laughing brightly as Ada heard her brothers' footsteps pounding up the staircase to their shared bedchamber. The other belonged to Ada and Elijah. A luxury that she did not mind one bit.

She turned as Elijah entered, and her smile widened. "How was your day, love?"

"Chaotic." He grinned and walked towards her, lifting his hands to her face. "But I wouldn't have it any other way."

"They don't need a scolding, then?"

He shook his head. "Not today." Slowly, he dipped his head and pressed his lips to hers. Smiling against his mouth, she looped her arms around his neck and nestled closer to his protective body.

"I missed you," she murmured, pulling away slightly.

"I missed you, too, even though I was only one door away." He laughed softly and turned his attention to the cradle in the corner of the kitchen. "How's the little one?"

Ada followed him to the cradle. "He's been smiling all day. I never knew I could lose so much time, just staring at a child, and the wonder of him."

"He's the most perfect child I could've asked for, because he's yours and mine. He could be a little monster and I would still think he's the sweetest child in the world," Elijah said, as he picked up the baby's rattle and shook it gently in front of the little boy's face. Baby John's plump hands reached for it: his eyes wide with determination. "Fortunately, he's an angel."

Ada rested her hand on the small of Elijah's back. "I love you, and I love our home, and our family." She cleared her throat, feeling suddenly choked up. "I'd have none of it if it weren't for you."

"And I'd have nothing if it weren't for you." He set down the rattle and pulled Ada into his arms, holding her close. "Every day that I get to spend with you, and your brothers, and our dear, sweet John is better than the last. I love you so very much, my Ada. More than I can put into words."

She giggled into his chest. "I think those words will do just fine."

Looking down at her baby boy, she knew there was no space for the past in their lives. They had only their present and their future, and a lifetime of happiness ahead of her. Thanks to Elijah, and the hope and patience and love he had given her, the wounds upon her heart had finally learned how to heal.

THE END

~ ~ ~ ~ ~

While this story is to mostly fictional, and the names are fictional, certain parts of the story are heavily based on the account of a real person who was hoodwinked by an unscrupulous character, drugged and sold into human trafficking. Much of the narrative of Ada's time in the brothel, is based on that account. And, later, she was taken into the home of the man who initially drugged her, where he kept there as his mistress. He did after a time, put her out onto the streets, with only the dress she was wearing, in favour of a younger woman.

In the actual account of what happened to this young woman, she never saw her family again, and remained a prostitute.

~~ ~~ ~

I hope that you enjoyed this book.

If you are willing to leave a short and honest review for me on Amazon, it will be very much appreciated, as reviews help to get my books noticed.

Over the page you will find a preview of one of my other books

The Little Chimney Sweep Girl

Join my newsletter and receive Victorian Romances only available to my valued subscribers.

PREVIEW

The Little Chimney Sweep Girl

Nell Harte

Part One

Chapter One

Elsie Grant's toes were so cold that she could barely feel them. She wrapped her fingers tightly around them, which didn't help much.

Her hands were almost as cold as her feet, which were bare, just like everything else in this tiny tenement: the raw floorboards that occasionally stuck dirty slivers under

Elsie's skin; the sleeping pallet where she was sitting; the square table in the middle of the floor; the cold hearth; the feeble glow of the few sticks of firewood.

It was hardly enough to warm the room at all, and definitely not enough to light it much. Shadows lurked in all of the corners, soaking the silvered cobwebs and grimy walls in darkness.

Elsie decided to try rubbing her feet a little. Perhaps that would warm them. Outside, winter thrashed in its death-throes, throwing vengeful gusts of wind against the walls. The bigger holes had been stopped up with rags and old newspapers, but there were still enough smaller gaps between the cheap bricks that Elsie could feel the draft running its icy fingertips across the back of her neck. Her feet still held the cold of the streets that she'd been wandering all day; she couldn't tell if the ache in her joints was hunger or exhaustion. Begging had proven unproductive, as it often did.

"I'm cold." The voice was small and reedy even when it wasn't pitched high in a whine, like it was now.

Elsie looked down at her five-year-old brother, Nick. His eyes were blue, and deep enough to drown in.

"Hush," Elsie whispered. She wrapped her arms around her brother's bony shoulders, tucking an edge of their threadbare blanket a little more tightly around his skeletal body.

"But I'm cold. And hungry," said Nick. "Why would no one give us anything today?"

"I'm also hungry," moaned two-year-old Gertie. Her mouth flopped loosely around the word, so that it came out more like *huggy*.

"Shh. We'll have supper later," said Elsie.

"But I'm hungry now."

"Gertie, hush!" Elsie hissed. She pulled the little girl into her lap with her free arm, feeling a pang of nervousness. "Don't make such a fuss. You'll bother Mama."

"When is Mama going to give us supper?" moaned Nick.

"Hush!" Elsie realized her voice was rising and swallowed hard, hoping Mama and her visitor hadn't heard. She pulled both siblings a little closer and rubbed them. "Mama will be out soon," she whispered under her breath. "Then she'll make us something nice for supper, and we'll have a good warm sleep."

"We never have something nice for supper," Gertie whimpered.

Elsie wanted to contradict her, but the gnawing hunger that tore at her belly was a brutal reminder of the truth.

She was trying to think of something to say when there were footsteps from the adjoining room. The children all huddled back on their pallet. Elsie felt the bones of her spine pressing against the wall, the bricks rough and harsh through her threadbare dress.

All three children kept their eyes glued to the narrow doorway in the opposite wall. Instead of a door, an old sheet — stained and moth-eaten — had been hung over the gap.

It was swept aside now by a great, thick-fingered hand covered in black hair, and an equally thick, hairy man stepped out of their mother's room.

His shaggy mane hung over his eyes, and he swayed a little as he walked, a familiar, fruity stench rolling from him.

His bare shoulders glittered with sweat as he grossed the room, mercifully ignoring the children, to where his coat was hanging on a hook near the front door. Tossing it over his shoulders, he shoved the door open and disappeared into the hallway.

The door gaped open in his wake. Elsie heard him laughing and singing, his words vague and slurred, all the way down the stairs to the door that led out onto the street.

"Mama," cried Nick. "Mama, we're so cold and hungry!"

Their mother had stepped out from behind the sheet. She wore a shapeless, colourless slip that slumped hopelessly around her wasted shoulders and narrow hips. Elsie could see the deep hollows under her collarbones; her eyes looked just as dark and empty. She said nothing to Nick, going over to the door to pull it quietly shut.

"Mama?" Elsie whispered.

Mama sighed, turning to them. Her voice was flat and tired. "How many times have I told you children to be quiet while I'm working?"

"We were quiet, Mama," said Gertie.

"Don't talk back to me." The words sounded like they should have been spat, but Mama spoke them without emotion.

"I'm sorry, Mama." Elsie stood up, letting the blanket fall down between her siblings, and picked her way over to her mother.

Mama's hands were limp by her sides; Elsie gripped them, but Mama failed to respond, gazing at Elsie with eyes like empty windowpanes. "I tried my best," Elsie whispered.

Mama pulled her hands away. "Why are you hungry?" she asked wearily. "Why didn't you go out begging like I told you?"

"I did," said Elsie. "Oh, I tried, Mama, I tried, but no one would even give us a crust of bread today."

"We're so hungry," Gertie whispered.

Mama's shoulders slumped, as if the toddler's words weighed on them like lead. "Sit down," she said.

Elsie half wished Mama would shout at her. Then at least she'd know that her mother still had feelings at all. She crept back to her pallet, and Mama went over to the wooden box in the corner. Pushing its lid aside, she retrieved a loaf of brown bread. It looked a little stale, but Elsie couldn't take her eyes off it as Mama approached the children and sat on the floor with a little groan of effort.

She broke the bread into four rough pieces, handing one to each of the children. Elsie tried her best not to snatch hers; Gertie was not as restrained, and crumbs spilled down the front of her baggy dress.

The bread was dry, but Elsie tore at it with her fingers, careful not to waste a single crumb. It felt so good sliding down into her stomach, which had been aching with emptiness. It wasn't long before hers was all gone; Nick's and Gertie's too, although Mama took some time picking at hers. The children knew better than to talk when she was eating.

When Mama's bread was all gone, Gertie piped up. "Mama, I'm still hungry."

"That's all there is." Again Mama's voice was tired, lifeless. Her eyes rested on Elsie's. "There's not enough for everyone anymore."

~ ~ ~ ~ ~

Elsie couldn't understand why Nick and Gertie weren't allowed to come.

When Mama shook her awake that morning, she'd been a little frightened. Mama never woke them; in fact, Mama seldom awoke this early herself, because she often worked late into the night. Elsie had asked what was wrong, but Mama hadn't responded. She'd just pulled Elsie out from between the sleeping forms of her siblings, wrapped her in an old pillowcase, and hustled her out of the tenement.

"Mama, what about Nick and Gertie?" she asked plaintively as they reached the front door leading out into the street. "We can't leave them at home alone all day. And why are you coming? You never come begging with us."

"We're not going begging," said Mama. "Come on." She stepped out into the street, Elsie close behind.

One time, one of Mama's callers – a rich man with a loud voice – had given the children a book with pictures in it. The pictures had been of trees and rolling hills and winding lanes and deep, limpid ponds.

Elsie wasn't sure what the book said, but she'd always assumed that the pictures were of heaven. She knew that the world looked nothing like those pictures.

On either side of the slushy, trampled path that served as a street here, buildings huddled, bent double and miserable. There were tenement houses like their own with multiple floors, teetering dangerously.

In between them there were squat little shelters made with bits of wood and old rags. The slush, which was everywhere, was a dispirited greyish brown, with odd yellow stains that made Elsie's stomach churn. A scrawny cat, missing one ear, paused halfway across the street as Mama slammed the door shut. Its coat clung to a skeletal frame, but it was one of the lucky ones.

The rotting remains of a less lucky feline lay next to the road, ignored, just like the pair of tramps sitting on the corner and watching Mama and Elsie with listless eyes.

She looked back over her shoulder at the tiny, high window of their tenement room. "Can we go back to Nick and Gertie now?" she asked. "We can't leave them alone."

"No." Mama gripped Elsie's arm; her hand was soft, but Elsie still wished Mama would hold her hand instead. "Come on."

Mama set off down the street at a brisk pace. Still wrapped in her pillowcase, Elsie had no option but to follow, even though she didn't want to go past the dead cat (which smelled bad) or the tramps (who smelled worse).

She couldn't understand why Mama was dragging her off like this.

She'd always been told to go and find her own way on the streets, with Nick and Gertie alongside. Some days, she had dreamed of walking the streets with Mama instead, of never being parted from her safe presence. But now that Mama really was with her, the cold look on her face was frightening Elsie.

"Where are we going?" Elsie asked, shivering a little.

"Walk faster. You'll be warmer," said Mama. She didn't answer Elsie's question.

It didn't take long before they left the familiar streets behind, and Elsie even began to hope that maybe they were going to escape from this dank part of the world completely. Yet Shoreditch seemed to stretch on endlessly, and Elsie's legs grew so cold and numb that she no longer cared where they were walking, as long as they could stop soon.

The wind stabbed sleet at Elsie's skin, and no matter where she looked, the streets were all the same: stinking of despondence and neglect. She kept having to look down to make sure that she wasn't stepping in any of the blobs of foul, nameless sludge that littered the muddy street.

Her legs were growing unbearably tired, and she was trying to pluck up the courage to ask Mama for a rest, when Mama turned sharply down a side street. The houses here looked a little different. They were smaller, for a start. Most of them had glass in the windowpanes; none of them looked like they were about to fall over.

The chimneys fascinated Elsie most. They looked similar to the chimneys of the streets she knew, but there was one difference. Near her home, the chimneys always had sad little wisps of smoke coming out of them. But here, the smoke came out in fat, bubbly clouds.

Mama marched up to one of the houses and let go of Elsie's arm. Raising a bony fist, she rapped on the bare wood of the front door. Straining her ears, Elsie thought she could hear voices from inside, but they were drowned out by the stomp of feet approaching. The door swung open, and Elsie looked up into a wide, red face.

She'd seen her fair share of men, enough that she could always tell which ones were going to leave Mama crying, and which would bring her presents and maybe even smile at the children. This man wasn't like any of them. He had clear blue eyes, pale as ice; his thick hair was the colour of straw, and there was a friendly little turn to the corner of his mouth. Next to him, Mama looked paler and more faded than ever.

"Are you Cooper?" she asked.

The man nodded. "Yes, ma'am, I'm Cedric Cooper." He looked down at Elsie, and kindness glinted in his eyes. "Is this the little one?"

"Yes," said Mama. "She's eight years old. Well-behaved. How much?"

Mr. Cooper tugged at his earlobe for a moment, his eyes turning contemplative. "She's a little slip of a thing," he said. "I'll give you five shillings."

Mama laughed, even though there was no humour in her face. "Do you take me for a fool? I know that any master sweep will pay at least ten for an eight-year-old child."

"She's a girl, though," Mr. Cooper pointed out. "She's not as strong as a boy."

"But she can't get soot wart, and she'll stay small for longer than a boy," Mama countered. "Ten shillings."

Mr. Cooper shook his head. "Six."

"Eight."

"Seven, and that's all you'll get." Mr. Cooper stuck out a shovel-sized hand to Mama.

Mama stared at him for a moment, then nodded and shook his hand. Mr. Cooper plucked a wallet out of his pocket and pulled out a few small, shiny coins, which he tipped into Mama's palm. She closed her hand over the money quickly, snatching it into her pocket as if she was afraid to lose it.

"Thank you," she said, turning away. Elsie went to follow her, but a huge, warm hand descended on the top of her head, stopping her.

"Now, now, little one," said Mr. Cooper.

"Let me go!" Elsie yelped. Mama was heading down the street, and a stab of fear lanced through Elsie's body. "Mama!" she screamed, squirming out of Mr. Cooper's grasp and lunging after Mama. "MAMA!"

Mr. Cooper seized her arm, effortlessly yanking her back. He didn't squeeze hard, but his hand engulfed her entire forearm, stopping her in her tracks. "Mama! Help!" Elsie shrieked.

She saw her words reach Mama; her shoulders flinched as if Elsie's scream had lashed over them like a whip. But Mama didn't turn back. She didn't come running to snatch Elsie from her captor. She just walked on, her head held high.

"Mamaaaa!" Elsie screamed.

"Hush, hush. Hush now," said Mr. Cooper. "She's not coming back, little one."

His voice was so gentle that Elsie looked up at him, feeling tears cooling on her cheeks. "Why not, sir?" she croaked.

"You're mine now," said Mr. Cooper. "But don't cry. Dry your tears and come inside – you look like you need a bite to eat."

He half led, half dragged Elsie toward the open front door, and she knew better than to fight him. Besides, his voice was so gentle, and she was hungry. Still, she couldn't stop staring and staring down the street until Mama had turned a corner and vanished.

Carrying her seven shillings, and leaving her daughter behind.

~ ~ ~ ~ ~

Mr. Cooper's cottage smelt of two things: soot, and boiling broth.

It was the broth that caught Elsie's attention immediately as Mr. Cooper led her through a little hallway and into a perfectly glorious kitchen.

There was a little round table in the middle of the stone floor; a fire roared on one side of the room, and there was a coal stove on the other. The broth smell came from that direction. A huge pot of something savoury bubbled on the stove, stirred vigorously by a comfortable woman in a grey wool dress that looked so thick and warm that Elsie wanted to roll herself up in it.

"Here you are, Linda," said Mr. Cooper, one hand still firmly on Elsie's shoulder. "We've got a new one. And she looks hungry."

The woman looked up. Her face was plain, with a nose that looked like it had been pressed roughly from a ball of dough, but her brown eyes seemed to fill Elsie with warmth as if they were windows of sunshine. "Oh, just look at you!" she cried, putting down her spoon and wiping her hands on her apron as she came over. "What a scrawny little mite you are. What's your name?"

"P-Elsie," she whispered under her breath.

"That's a beautiful name. Did you know that poppies are the most wonderful red flowers?" Mrs. Cooper reached out and took Elsie's hand, the way Elsie had wished Mama would.

"Now, I'm going to introduce you to the other children, and I'll bring you some nice soup in a minute. It's nearly ready."

Other children? Elsie nodded, meekly allowing Mrs. Cooper to lead her across the room. She wondered if their mamas had sold them too. If their mamas thought that they were worth less than a few bits of dead metal.

Mrs. Cooper led her down a series of steps and to a narrow little door that made Elsie's heart thump hard. She didn't like the feeling of being underground, but her fear was quickly dispelled when Mrs. Cooper pushed the door open.

The cellar was nothing like the nasty, stinky one under the tenement building that Elsie had seen on the many occasions that Mama wanted to hide her and her siblings from some gentleman caller. That place had been cold and very dark. This one was filled with light.

Oil lamps burned in every corner, and a boiler in the back filled the room with warmth. Straw beds were lined up in three neat rows down the middle, and a circle of children sat on them, facing each other with their hands up. It looked like they'd been frozen in the middle of a game. Most of them had joy on their faces.

"Maggie, darling," said Mrs. Cooper, "this is Elsie. She'll be joining us and learning our trade."

Elsie felt suddenly shy as a battery of inquisitive looks focused on her. The children seemed to be all a little older than she was; most of them were boys, but there were two or three girls. The biggest one got to her feet and came over.

She had a beautiful, warm smile that lifted the mole on the corner of her lip, and a cascade of mousy curls spilling over her shoulders.

"Hello, Elsie love," she said. "I'm Maggie. You don't have to be afraid." And without any ceremony, she scooped Elsie up into her arms and set her down on her hip. Automatically, Elsie wound her hands around Maggie's neck; her skin was warm, and her hair very soft where it touched Elsie's arms. Maggie carried her over to one of the beds and sat on it, keeping Elsie cradled in her lap, as Mrs. Cooper left.

"Your hair is so pretty," Elsie whispered, staring at it.

"Yours will be very pretty too after we've given it a good wash on Sunday afternoon," said Maggie, smiling back at her. She lifted a strand of Elsie's oily black hair and rubbed it between her fingers.

"I hope it's not cold on Sunday," said Elsie.

"Oh, Mrs. Cooper washes us with lovely warm water," said Maggie. She kissed Elsie's forehead. "Don't you be afraid now, my sweet. We work hard here, but the Coopers take good care of us. You'll never go to bed hungry while you're here. Or cold, either."

"Did your mama sell you?" Elsie asked.

Maggie wrapped her arms tight around Elsie and held her close. "It doesn't matter here," she said. "Try not to think about it."

But even with Maggie's kindness throbbing against her as steadily as the heartbeat Elsie heard when she nestled into the older girl's chest, she could think of nothing else.

READ THE REST

Subscribe to Nell Harte's newsletter and receive Subscriber only books.